FROSTFIRE

FROSTFIRE
EILA'S EXILE™
BOOK THREE

D.S. BAILEY
MICHAEL ANDERLE

This book is a work of fiction. All of the characters, organizations, and events portrayed in this novel are either products of the author's imagination or are used fictitiously. Sometimes both.

Copyright © 2025 LMBPN Publishing
Cover by Mihaela Voicu http://www.mihaelavoicu.com/
Cover copyright © LMBPN Publishing
A Michael Anderle Production

LMBPN Publishing supports the right to free expression and the value of copyright. The purpose of copyright is to encourage writers and artists to produce the creative works that enrich our culture.

The distribution of this book without permission is a theft of the author's intellectual property. If you would like permission to use material from the book (other than for review purposes), please contact support@lmbpn.com. Thank you for your support of the author's rights.

LMBPN® Publishing
2375 E. Tropicana Avenue, Suite 8-305
Las Vegas, Nevada 89119 USA

Version 1.01, April 2025
ebook ISBN: 979-8-88878-975-9
Print ISBN: 979-8-89354-424-4

THE FROSTFIRE TEAM

Thanks to the JIT Readers

Sean Kesterson
Zacc Pelter
Diane L. Smith
Dave Hicks
Dorothy Lloyd
Paul Westman
Jan Hunnicutt

If I've missed anyone, please let me know!

Editor
The SkyFyre Editing Team

PROLOGUE

The ground trembled. Alarms blared.

There was a knock on the door.

"Your Majesty! Your Majesty!" someone called.

Queen Amara sat by a window, looking out at her kingdom. The sky was clear, the world white and blue. Far below, in the courtyards and passages within the palace walls, Winter Fae were slowing, staring up at something out of the queen's sight.

"Your Majesty!" the person exclaimed. "It's an emergency!"

Queen Amara inhaled, then looked over her shoulder. Her back was straight. No emotion showed on her beautiful face. "Enter."

The knob twisted. Bryce Sleetwing, one of the queen's Seven, entered the room with a haunted expression on his face.

"What is it?" Queen Amara crooned, exuding power as cries and footsteps rang in the halls. "It must be important to disturb my morning meditation."

Bryce bowed. "My apologies, your Majesty. I come bearing grave news."

The disturbance spread quickly, and shouts erupted outside the window.

"It has been taken," Queen Amara stated flatly. That had been clear when it happened. She sensed its absence, as though a dam had cracked and drained her abilities.

"It has," Bryce confirmed. "Moments ago. Your soldiers are hunting for the thief before they leave the palace and escape into the wilds."

"Do you know who you are looking for?" Queen Amara muttered, turning her attention back to the window. Fae were gathering in the market square, filling the alleys and lanes surrounding it.

Bryce shifted uneasily.

"Master Sleetwing," Amara nudged.

Bryce cleared his throat. "We have our suspicions."

Queen Amara narrowed her eyes, then sighed. She had seen this event in her dreams and in the mirror on her dressing table. Although she had hoped it would not come to pass, she had understood that it would. She could only hope that the chess pieces were playing their parts. Queen Amara's influence stretched far and wide, but she could not control destiny.

"He is gone, then?" Queen Amara asked coolly.

Bryce frowned. "He left his chamber, Your Majesty. No one has seen him since before the dawn."

Queen Amara nodded. The sky that had only a moment ago been clear now contained roiling dark clouds. A bright purple flash snaked across the sky as the first drop that signified a melting kingdom slid down the window.

"And so it begins," Queen Amara muttered. "The end game. We will trust the Mother and hope she saves us all."

"Excuse me, Your Majesty?" Bryce asked.

Queen Amara turned her cold stare on him. Rising so suddenly that her gown swooshed around her feet, she bellowed, *"Assemble the scouts! Take to the sky!"*

Bryce turned to leave.

"Sleetwing," Amara added. Bryce withered under her glare.

"Keep silent. Let the peasants guess what is happening. We cannot lose our grip on this situation. Do you understand?"

Bryce nodded.

"Go." She waved Bryce away and turned back to the window. The clouds were moving fast. She laced her fingers behind her back as Bryce's commands roused the troops. Three bands of scouts took to the sky, passing Amara's window as the hunt began.

In the dark recesses of her mind, Queen Amara conjured the vision that had haunted her dreams: a fierce duel of blue and red magic. A blizzard and a roar were the only way that it could end in victory.

She had to win, not just for her world but for the fate of all the known realms.

CHAPTER ONE

Sweat dripped off Eila's forehead as she crouched in front of a glass panel. Her knees complained. Heat pulsed from inside the large, square device.

A shadow loomed behind her, darkening the window. They were all burning, the tops turning black as goo overflowed and dripped onto the—

"Your oven is too hot," Karen admonished. She twisted the dial from two hundred and twenty degrees Celsius to its correct one hundred and eighty. "I told you what would happen."

"The sheet says three-fifty," Eila rebuked, combing a finger down the tattered page. Her heart dropped when she saw that the temperature was in Fahrenheit, not Celsius. "Shit."

"You didn't think to question that two-twenty was as high as your oven went?" Karen asked, folding her arms. "Also, I pre-heated the ovens. I don't know why you felt the need to mess with the dial."

She nodded at the range. "Go on, get them out. That's another fiver I'll have to put out for ingredients." She looked toward the front of the class, where a spare desk contained ingredients for someone who hadn't turned up that day. "You can use Caitlin's mix." She continued speaking as she walked away. "It's hard to mess up something as simple as a brownie."

Eila's cheeks flushed as she took the charred bars out. The top had turned black from the heat, and the batter had exploded out of the tray. She exchanged a glance with Leonie and stifled a laugh as Karen returned with the ingredients.

"Start again," Karen instructed. "Good thing these are quick. I can't wait to see what you'll turn out when we move on to pastries and meringue."

Eila filled another bowl with viscous brownie batter. While Karen focused on Bethany's masterpieces, Eila scraped a finger through the bowl and brought the chocolate deliciousness to her lips. She rolled her eyes when Leonie grinned at her.

Cleaning the pan was a nightmare. Eila spent five minutes in the back scrubbing off the scorched, blackened mess.

Karen admonished her for not understanding the magic of non-stick spray. Eila held the scrubber in one fist and slowly revealed the surface of the tray. Although it looked cleaner, Karen complained about the "arm and a leg" she would have to pay for a new one.

Ten minutes after everyone else had left, Eila retrieved her brownies from the oven. The room was empty except for Leonie. Karen had gone out to lunch, informing Eila that her next class would arrive in half an hour, but on this one occasion, she'd give Eila additional time to finish her bake.

"Those are brownies?" Leonie announced as Eila placed the pan on the work table.

Eila glanced at Leonie's confections, which were rectangular and uniform, with attractive dark brown bubbles on top.

Her batch was another disaster. The batter had risen higher in some places than others. In one corner, the mass was blackened and curled.

"Mother, why is this so hard?" Eila asked.

"Because you're new," Leonie replied matter-of-factly. "You can't expect to be great at everything yet. Was your magic perfect when you got here?"

Eila thought about her power's unreliability after she passed through the Faerie Door. Grimrock had mentioned that powers sometimes went awry upon arrival, especially if it was one's first trip to a new realm.

They had evened out. If only she could fix the nagging problem she had caused the night she arrived. Her thoughts flashed to Jim Spencer, miserable and locked up in his room after losing yet another job because of the truth-telling curse she had cast on him. *Now you know what it's like to be a faerie.*

"Did that happen to you, too?" Eila asked.

"The unpredictable powers or the awful bake?" Leonie replied.

"Both," Eila returned.

Leonie retrieved a knife from a nearby drawer. "Absolutely." She made long cuts, separating the solid block into smaller, even pieces. "You think I didn't burn things in the beginning? And I watched my mother for years and had decades of practice to prepare for this class. Marcus loves his birthday cakes, which are triple chocolate. I'm not saying they're fit for the windows of Patisserie Valerie, but he loves them."

Eila was impressed. There were brownies in the pan, not an amorphous lump.

"Take them out, and let's see what we're working with," Leonie instructed. "I'll show you some magic."

A few minutes later (and with half a dozen brownie segments stacked on a nearby plate), Eila had a stack of reasonably uniform brownies.

"The trick is in the presentation," Leonie stated. "Show these to your friends, and they won't care about the third of the mixture we discarded. They'll only see the good ones."

"That's cheating." Eila was torn between feeling good about the brownies that were okay or bad about the ones that were only fit for the trash can.

"That's *life*," Leonie replied to bolster Eila's spirits. "Stores, social media, or our friends, we only ever show the good. We rarely show the bad, the terrible, the painful. Answer me this: how many people in your life would you share everything with? I mean, *everything*."

Eila recalled the people she cared about most. Aria, though even she played the Winter Fae's games of avoiding the truth and subverting the bureaucracy.

Her father had been silent since Eila was banished.

Corvus and Grimrock were solid companions, though she was not ready to let them in on every dark and dusty corner of her life.

Fenris, Gizmo, and Ryker were stalwart comrades but not yet friends.

Lyrian, the object of her heart's desire, had fallen a few notches in her estimation over the last few days. She wanted to believe he was a force for good, but Corvus' and Grimrock's suspicions had stained Eila's opinion of the Summer Fae. Her heart still fluttered when she thought about his face, smell, and smile, but perhaps Lyrian wasn't as squeaky clean as she'd thought he was.

Who did that leave? The only person Eila had totally trusted was her mother, who would spend hours in Eila's room, describing her adventures and listening to her daughter's concerns. Eila's mother had been her rock, and both Eila and her father had found it difficult to cope with her passing. Even now, years after Eila had been forced to say goodbye at a funeral with no body in the casket, Eila could still feel the pain and the hole her mother had left behind.

Leonie smirked. "Your silence speaks volumes."

Eila blinked when Karen returned. "I told you to be gone when I got back."

Eila proudly held up the plate of good-looking brownies.

Karen barely glanced her way. "Great job. You've baked brownies. Now, if you don't mind, I'd like to eat my sandwich in peace before the next class arrives."

The sky was overcast as Eila and Leonie traversed the path that crossed Karen's pristine lawn. Eila's gaze lingered on the little pond with its trickling water feature. There were no frogs today. A sparrow stood awkwardly on a lily pad, cocking its head in all directions as it focused on something swimming beneath the water.

"I wonder why she's such an ass to you," Leonie pondered as they closed the gate behind them.

Eila laughed. "I have no idea. If you weren't in the class with me, I would have quit."

"She has no right," Leonie continued. "You're a great baker. You just need a little more…encouragement than the others."

Eila rolled her eyes. "You don't have to say that."

"Say what?" Leonie smirked. "You're amazing. The hottest baker this side of Soho. Better than Pru. Better than Paul. You know what? She's lucky to have you in that class."

Eila batted Leonie's arm. "All right, you made your point, even if you are lying through your teeth."

Leonie laughed, rubbing her arm. "Seriously, you're doing well, and I need someone in the class I can tolerate."

"You mean someone who makes you look good."

"Was that what I said?" Leonie returned with a smile.

They laughed until a loud engine captured Eila's attention. She scanned for black motorcycle ridden by people in black armor. Several days had passed since her last encounter with the Oathkeepers, but she hadn't lowered her guard.

Leonie eyed Eila. "You want a ride home?"

Eila waved a hand. "I'm okay. You're going in the opposite direction, and isn't it hot yoga today?" Eila's cheeks got warm as she recalled bending herself into knots as air in the room attempt to melt her from the inside out. She believed she knew what her first brownies had felt like.

"Not today," Leonie replied. "Life painting this time. Can't wait to get my eyes on some wrinkled human balls."

Eila was taken aback, and her mouth fell open.

Laughing, Leonie added, "Humans do weird shit, all right? I just want to see what the class is like."

"A class where you paint *naked* humans?"

"You interested?"

"Mother, no!" Eila returned. Another loud engine drew her attention. "Look, I have to go. I promised Corvus I'd come straight back after class. We've got things to talk about."

Leonie's eyes glinted. "You do?"

"Not like that," Eila replied exasperatedly. "We're just friends. I told you that."

"Mmm," Leonie replied evasively. "Well, you don't want to keep him waiting." She strode to her car, waving over her shoulder. "Say hi to lover boy for me!"

Eila turned away as a black motorcycle sped past, the rider wearing a red and white helmet and crimson leathers. He did a double-take at Eila as he passed, then sped on his way.

Eila walked in the opposite direction.

CHAPTER TWO

"*You* made these?" Corvus asked Eila. They were sitting by the warm fire in the Green Dragon.

He examined a brownie and tossed it into his mouth whole. Ecstasy flooded his face as he chewed. Eila laughed, and several patrons turned around curiously.

"Delicious," Corvus managed. "You nailed it. You best put the cover on those or I'm going to keep grabbing them."

Eila smirked. "I thought you had better control."

"Not for sweet things," Corvus returned. His gaze flicked to a vampire who stood at the bar with a thick gold watch on his wrist.

"Or shiny things," Eila added.

It felt strange to sit beside Corvus and shoot the shit after recent occurrences. Eila had only been in London for a few weeks, and the things she had predicted might happen had not. When she'd stepped through the Faerie Door and seen London, she had envisioned a quiet life in which she fought to remain anonymous and experience living among humans.

She hadn't predicted befriending a ravenkin, finding a home with an ancient troll, and joining a local revolutionary force that had helped her uncover a child trafficking ring that almost shattered the Oath of Realms and brought about a second darkness.

It was wild to think that only a few days had passed since she had been in an earlier London beneath the city, fighting hordes of gloamhounds as Fenris and his merry gang attempted to thwart the plans of a corrupted faerie. This morning, she had taken a cooking class and screwed up the recipe for brownies.

She glanced at Corvus. The ravenkin was refreshed after a few days off but white patches had appeared on the sides of his head. She remembered their conversation after they left Fenris' Nemora to return to Under the Bridge and find Grimrock.

The city had been quiet in the golden glow of early morning, though they'd had to evade two patrolling groups of Oathkeepers en route to Corvus' home. When they arrived, they flew onto the roof and sat on the edge.

Eila leaned back on her hands, the sunlight dazzling her as it penetrated the slits between skyscrapers. Across the city were the Gherkin, the Eye, and the O2, all testaments to architectural genius as rich men and women fought to leave their legacy on London's skyline.

"What a night," Corvus offered, squinting at the rising sun. "What. A. Night."

Eila nodded and idly reached for the crown that was no longer on her head. She had returned it to Fenris. "You can say that again."

"Three times?" Corvus quipped.

"Don't." Eila replayed the evening's events in her head. It had all seemed so frantic, and everything had happened so fast. There was still much she didn't know about this world and its neighboring realms, as well as about those closest to her. "Are you going to tell me what happened back there?"

The mirth left Corvus' face. "You're asking about my magic?"

"No," Eila replied sarcastically. "I'm asking about the water feature that runs through underground London."

Corvus frowned. "I don't know what to tell you."

"Maybe start with where the hell you've been hiding your abilities," Eila returned. "It's not like we haven't been in scrapes before. Liza's den. The yacht. Where was that in those situations?"

Corvus looked at his knees. "It's not that simple, Eila. The ravenkin are cursed. Our magic is—"

"Brilliant?" Eila interrupted. "Powerful? Awesome?"

"Painful." Corvus met Eila's gaze, discomfort in his eyes.

"'Painful?'"

Corvus pulled up his sleeve, revealing bruises and darkened veins beneath his skin.

Eila grabbed his arm and Corvus winced, resisting slightly as she pulled it closer. It looked as though his blood had turned to ink. Some bruises were yellow, and Corvus grimaced as he moved his fingers. His index finger crooked like arthritis had claimed it. "Oh, Mother! I didn't realize..."

Corvus drew his arm back and pulled the sleeve down, hiding the evidence. "It's a blessing and a curse. I can only use them sparingly, like all ravenkin. Why wouldn't the queen punish us for using our incredible abilities?"

Eila thought about seeing the darkness enshroud his enemies. "You didn't have to. You could've stayed back and..."

"No, I couldn't." His gaze locked with Eila's. Eila studied the lines of his lips. Corvus leaned toward her, and Eila melted...

Fluttering feathers broke the spell: a pigeon speeding past them as it dashed into the dawn sky.

Eila turned back to the sunrise. "Well, thank you."

Corvus ran his fingers through his hair. "What makes you think I did it for you?"

Eila rolled her eyes, but her gaze drifted back to his lips and the chiseled lines of his jaw.

"You'd think that after everything we've been through, Boulderboy would have broken out of his shell a little. Become more of a conversationalist," Corvus mused. He spoke loudly to draw the attention of the golem at the nearby table.

Eila blinked. The beverage was almost too hot to drink, but the hot chocolate was sweet enough to distract her.

Boulderbeast gripped his large tankard as the patrons chattered around him. Corvus held up Eila's Tupperware container. "You want one? They're good. I vouch for them."

Boulderbeast didn't move.

"Leave him alone," Eila ordered, then popped a brownie into her mouth. Corvus was right; they weren't half bad.

Ryker appeared. Eila caught the centaur's scent, and her worries evaporated. "You *have* to tell me which aftershave you use. You'd make a killing on meditative retreats."

"Aftershave?" Ryker grinned and changed the subject. "He's ready for you, if you'll follow me."

Eila chuckled. "We can use the front door this time?"

Ryker glanced at the nearby tables to ensure no one was eavesdropping and lowered his voice. "We don't advise the alternate routes. Most who try are never seen again, my lady. Only a lucky few make the Governor's acquaintance."

"Roger, Roger," Corvus replied, putting another brownie in his mouth. Eila shut the lid and handed the box to Noddle to place behind the bar.

"Lead the way," Eila instructed.

"You're not offering one to Ryker?" Corvus asked.

Ryker grinned and turned away.

"Fair enough," Corvus muttered. He shot a glance at Boulderbeast, who remained stoic.

"Splash yourself with the water from the pool if you want to," Ryker offered.

They had just reached the rushing falls and the Crystal Pool. The moon, still impossibly large and full, hung in the sky like a prop in a theater production. That was the only thing that felt familiar about the trail through Nemora.

As they journeyed down the wooded path, Eila would have sworn the trees had changed. The trunks were lighter, and the leaves were less green and had more orange patches. The path wound in directions that didn't fit with Eila's memory of this place, and on more than a couple of occasions, they passed rock formations she thought she would have remembered.

In one formation in a hollow, the protruding rocks were like the fingers of a stone giant buried beneath the earth. On top of some of the stones, owls and ravens perched, watching Eila and Corvus with glinting eyes as they passed.

"What is this place?" Eila asked in awe.

Ryker trotted a few steps ahead. "You've asked that before."

"But it's different," Eila looked at Corvus for confirmation. He nodded.

"It is what it needs to be," Ryker returned. "The Governor's illusory magic is strong, and Nemora responds to his moods, patterns, and shifting ways of thinking. You can learn a lot about the Governor by observing the changes if you spend enough time with him."

"What does this tell you?" Corvus asked, motioning at the trees and rocks.

Ryker paused. "The Governor is troubled."

Eila crouched beside the pool and scooped up some water with her hands. When she splashed her face, the chill made her gasp as it worked its magic on her. Her eyes got brighter, and the day's aches and tiredness washed away.

"Corvus?" Ryker offered, motioning to the water.

Corvus eyed it with suspicion. "I'm okay."

Eila's gaze flicked to his arms. "Do it, Corvus. It'll be good for you."

Though she hadn't seen the injuries from his magic for a few days, she thought he was still suffering.

Corvus' lips thinned. "I'm good."

Eila blocked his path. "Please? For me."

Corvus sighed and glanced at Ryker, then at the pool. He crouched and drew up the sleeves of his jacket to reveal muscled forearms with traces of black beneath the skin.

Corvus hesitated before plunging his hands into the pool, then splashed his face. A lock of hair got wet and fell in a Superman curl. He started to stand, but Ryker put a hand on his shoulder.

"Dip your arms," the centaur instructed.

Corvus grimaced, then slipped his arms into the pool. He winced, though from actual pain or imagined, it was hard to tell. The ink in his veins filtered through the skin and dispersed into the pool, creating a black cloud in the water. It hovered for a moment before being sucked into the heart of the pool and out of sight.

Corvus stood and examined his arms. His veins had returned to their normal color and were barely visible beneath the skin.

"Better?" Ryker asked.

Corvus shrugged. "We'll see."

Sensing Corvus' stubbornness, Ryker did not press it. He led them through the magical tunnel beneath the waterfall and into Fenris' workshop.

Fenris was waiting for them, as were Thrumble, Finn, Gizmo, and…

"Boulderbeast?" Eila asked incredulously, wondering how the golem had beaten them here.

Corvus' gaze flicked between Boulderbeast and Eila.

"Eila. Corvus. Nice of you to join us," Fenris announced, indicating the seats they should take. "I've got news to share that affects all of us."

Eila took the indicated seat. Corvus shifted his closer to her. His scent was distracting as she tried to focus on the matter at hand.

"What is it?" Corvus asked. "Got another occult fae fucking shit up and carting kiddos through the Faerie Door? How is ol' Maevis, by the way?"

Eila had been wondering the same thing. After converting Maevis back to her original form, they had taken her to Nemora. Maevis had been asleep or unconscious the whole way back, and Fenris had informed them he would take care of her in a hidden facility. "A safe space for her to recuperate before we decide what to do with her."

His answer had been vague, but Eila and Corvus had been too tired to argue. They hadn't seen her since.

"She's recovering," Fenris answered flatly. "We are treating her well, and we probe every day to see if she remains dangerous." A shadow flitted across his face. "It is partly because of this that I have gathered you all here."

His gaze has an intensity Eila hadn't seen in Fenris before when he turned to her. "Perhaps you most of all."

CHAPTER THREE

All eyes turned to Eila. The room fell quiet.

"Me?" Eila asked, hand on her chest. "Why me?"

Fenris worried his lip with his teeth, studying Eila. "There has been some disruption in your former home. In-fighting among the palace residents. Security breaches. The turmoil is not being discussed but appears to be creating wide-ranging ripples through the realms. We need intel."

Eila frowned. "What does that have to do with me? I was banished, and I can't go back on pain of death. This is my home now, so I'm not sure what I can do."

Gizmo squeaked, "You know the lay of the land and the people. You have information that no one here can access."

"Send a scout," Eila commanded. "You must have eyes and ears on the inside who can funnel information to you."

Fenris shook his head. "We couldn't penetrate the Winter Court. Your people are mistrusting, suspicious, blunt, and cruel."

"Don't mince words." Eila rolled her eyes.

"Breaking into a place like that would take years or even decades," Fenris continued. "You know that better than anyone else. You thrived in that environment. You *know* the court."

"I do... Well, I *did*," Eila corrected. "What of it? I can't go back."

"And we're not asking you to," Fenris stated. "*I'm* not asking you to. I was hoping that you might know a way for us to gain this intel. A contact or a means to gain information from the palace. Perhaps you're still in touch with someone on that side of the door, and they've heard about the upset."

Eila's stomach roiled as she posed the question, "What *is* happening over there?"

Fenris sat back, exchanging glances with Gizmo. Thrumble, Finn, and Boulderbeast watched the discourse like spectators at a tennis match.

"Simply put? Destruction," Fenris explained. "We have heard rumors of crops dying, in-fighting among your kin, and the queen's soldiers raiding houses and scouring the land for something that they will not describe. As the chaos grows, your people are struggling to keep it under wraps. I have heard reports from the Autumn Court that the same is happening there. Fields are yielding less. Strange, dark folk have been seen. Something is stirring, Eila, and we need to know what."

Eila thought hard for a moment. "That is how my mother described the beginning of the Great Cataclysm. A slow decay that became chaotic."

Fenris nodded again. The room was pregnant with expectation and tension, and it was too warm.

Eila wiped her brow. "We stopped Maevis, and we prevented the breaking of the Oath of Realms. Didn't we?"

Fenris leaned forward, not blinking his yellow eyes. "So I believe. But something is afoot, and it begins and ends with the Winter Court. That I'm certain of."

Eila sat back in her chair, glancing around the table as she racked her brain for information that might be useful to these revolutionaries. For a moment, she was in the underground city again, standing before the portal as Maevis attempted to funnel the children through. Her magic had been too powerful for Eila until she activated the Harvest Crown.

Eila had run through the Faerie Door and dragged the children back before they crossed into Faerie, but what if…

What if the Oath of Realms had been broken when they passed through the first portal? What if they *had* been too late?

We would have known before now. Wouldn't breaking the Oath of Realms affect every race that signed the proclamation, and wouldn't it all happen at once, not just in the Winter Court?

"I am not alone in this journey," Maevis jeered in Eila's memory. "And I will not sit solo on the throne. Once he has the Icicle Sceptre, the world will fall to shadow and bow to our command. It is inevitable."

Eila saw a page in an ancient text in Grimrock's library. *"That's a fascinating piece, isn't it?"* Corvus idly ran a finger over the illustration on the page.

The Icicle Sceptre. Could that be a part of this equation? Hadn't rumors been flying that Lyrian had attempted to steal the Sceptre, but he had been caught by…

Silas.

Thoughts raced through her mind. The table and her companions disappearing as she wrestled with her inner turmoil.

Rumor said that Lyrian had attempted to steal the Icicle Sceptre.

Silas *had* caught him sneaking around the halls.

She had no idea who to believe or what had really happened down there.

Grimrock had found something in those pages that caused him to go off on his own. Eila and Corvus hadn't seen him since that day, and they were worried about him.

Could it all be linked? Eila thought. *If somebody had successfully stolen the Icicle Sceptre…*

She was transported back to the Winter Court, sitting on her mother's knees in front of a blue-flame fire in the ice hearth, enchanted so that no heat save dragon fire could destroy what had taken so long to craft. Eila's father was in his office agonizing over official documents, as was his wont. On her mother's lap, Eila felt safe.

"The world is magic," Lysandra Snowshadow soothed, running her fingers through her daughter's hair. *"You find traces of it in the air, the trees, and the water."*

"In the walls?" Eila asked.

"Yes."

"In my belly?" Eila pointed at her pale stomach, which was visible beneath her scrunched top.

"Definitely." Lysandra poked Eila's belly button, causing her to explode in laughter. *"Especially in your belly. You're special, Eila. You know that, don't you?"*

"I do," Eila confirmed, not really understanding. She stared at the fire. *"Why doesn't the fire melt the ice?"*

Lysandra smiled. "Because of the magic in the palace."

"What makes the magic?"

"We do," Lysandra replied. *"Our queen does. Our people. Our treasures."*

"Treasures?" Eila's mouth dropped open, her eyes bright as she looked at her mother. *"What treasures?"*

Lysandra had told Eila about a hidden treasure room containing an item so powerful it was the beating heart of the Winter Court. It had been created before recorded memory, and only the queen and her kin could wield a Sceptre so powerful that it maintained the palace's everwinter. It was linked to their people, so its removal could destroy the realm.

Had it been stolen?

"Eila?" Fenris drew Eila back.

Shaking her head, she glanced up. "The only explanation is that someone stole the heart of the palace." She didn't need to say the item's name.

Fenris' serious gaze confirmed her suspicions, and he took a deep breath.

Thrumble asked, "What is it?"

Corvus shot Eila a concerned glance. She looked down at the table.

Fenris rose and slowly walked around the table. "I will not say yet. I need confirmation"

Eila stiffened as Fenris passed behind her, his aura producing an almost physical force. "We need to find out the truth," Fenris stated.

"How do we do that?" Thrumble continued. "You said it yourself. The Winter Fae are a cruel bunch, and they don't open up to strangers. We need an ally on the inside, and none of us have one."

Fenris rested his hands on the back of his chair and glanced thoughtfully at the table. After a moment of silence, he announced, "You are dismissed."

For a beat, no one moved. Thrumble glanced at Finn, worried. Boulderbeast was the first to shift, rising mechanically and striding through the falls and out of sight. Thrumble and Finn followed him.

As Eila stood, Fenris locked eyes with her. "Please stay, Eila. We must talk further."

Corvus hesitated.

Fenris waited.

"Where she goes, I go," Corvus replied stubbornly.

Fenris met his gaze.

Eila placed a hand on his shoulder. "It's okay. I'll see you back at Grimrock's place."

Corvus searched Eila's eyes, threw an irritated glance at Fenris, and followed the others.

The door to Gizmo's workshop closed as the goblin disappeared into his lair.

Eila stood, fingers resting on the table, awaiting Fenris' next words.

"You're holding something back," Fenris accused. There was

no menace in it, only pity.

"I don't have the answer." Eila was skirting the truth, but it wasn't a lie.

Fenris sat down, steepling his fingers. "You spent most of your life there, Eila. There must be someone you can contact who can get us intel. It is of dire importance."

Eila sighed. "I know people, but as you said, my people are a bitter bunch. They generally cannot be trusted."

"Someone can be," Fenris stated.

Eila cocked her head. "What makes you certain?"

"*You* exist, Eila. People, races, and species have a million traits in common, but there are always exceptions. Thieves and bandits reside in the Summer Court. There is a centaur downstairs who has learned to live among humans. I live with a goblin with green fur who melts the hearts of those around him. There are *always* exceptions."

Eila played with her fingers, unsure of how to take the compliment.

"You are a Winter Fae, but you have a heart," Fenris continued. "You fight for others without reserve. You could be living an easy life by manipulating humans, but you are seeking justice. You are prepared to die for what is right."

"You assume a lot for someone who has spent very little time with me," Eila returned mildly.

"A miner recognizes a diamond among the rocks. You are special, and as a hopelessly romantic optimist, I believe you are not unique. There must be others in the court who will work toward a greater good. Looking into my eyes, tell me that you cannot think of a single ally in the court."

Eila held Fenris' hypnotic amber gaze. Whatever he was, the being had a power Eila couldn't comprehend.

Two Winter fae came to mind. She thought of her father, the squeaky-clean diplomat who was happy to climb the political ladder slowly. Calen Snowshadow was on her side, but his loyalty belonged firmly to the palace. He would not help the other realms.

The other was Aria Frostwind, her former ally. Aria was born the same year as Eila, and they had spent their childhood together. Aria had been a constant in her life, though not always a reliable shoulder to lean on. Aria had consoled Eila when her mother passed and had introduced Eila to Lyrian at the Summer Court Fete. Aria was as capable of turning on her for self-preservation as any Winter fae, but Eila had shared adventures with her friend and trusted her.

Hadn't Aria encouraged Eila to free Lyrian, sensing her love for the Summer fae? There had been no benefit to that, only a sincere longing to help a friend find love.

"You thought of someone," Fenris stated.

Eila nodded. "I did, though I do not know how to contact her from here."

Fenris drew a piece of parchment from his pocket, slid it across the table, and handed Eila a pen. "You write the words. I'll find the messenger."

Eila frowned. "I thought you couldn't access the Winter Court."

"We can get in." Fenris grinned. "We just can't gain trust or allies."

Eila nodded. She was to lure Aria into their company to draw out secrets. Eila would be a mole. "How can things change so quickly?" Eila shook her head as she composed the letter. When she was finished, she slid the paper back to Fenris. He popped it into an envelope, and Eila provided the address.

"Let's hope the truth comes as quickly," Fenris replied. "It has been many centuries since I was this concerned. I just hope we can prevent what I fear most."

"What is that?" Eila asked, though she knew the answer.

Fenris' face betrayed emotion. "An ending to all."

CHAPTER FOUR

Eila's heels clipped the sidewalk as she made her lonely way home. The wind was brisk, and rain darkened the ground. She wove down streets and past tall buildings, on edge as she glanced over her shoulder.

Someone's following me.

Several times, she turned sharply, peering into dark alleys and side streets, hoping to catch her pursuer.

Maybe I'm just paranoid. The talk of disruption and danger in Faerie has gotten to me. What place will be safe if the Faerie realms are turning on each other?

She ducked down a one-way street and passed the darkened windows of florists and bakers and lawyers and cobblers. As she neared the street's end, her pursuers revealed themselves.

A man in a black helmet stepped out ahead of her, blocking her path. Behind her were two more Oathkeepers. Eila ran her fingers through her hair. "I wondered where you guys had gone. It's been far too quiet these last few days."

They didn't reply. The keeper before her brandished a weapon that looked like a truncheon but produced blue electricity. Eila thought about her first encounter with these people and the power in their net that had caused her to black out.

That was the night she'd met Grimrock.

Where are you, buddy?

Eila raised placating hands. "Let's talk this through. Whatever you think I've done…"

Like escape their prison and run riot around London.

"I'm sure we can come to a compromise."

The two Oathkeepers behind her stepped forward. Eila wondered if they'd been tracking her, or if her luck had just run out. Either way, there was only one path to follow. "We don't have to do this."

The Oathkeeper in front of her hurled the truncheon at Eila. The projectile whistled toward her, leaving blue streaks of power behind it. Eila conjured a block of ice, and the truncheon impotently smacked into the barrier.

The Oathkeeper used the distraction to sprint forward, reaching into his pocket. The other two moved closer as well.

A gunshot rang out, and light flared in the street. The block of ice exploded into glittering fragments as the projectile penetrated the block right where she had been standing a moment before.

The first Oathkeeper skidded awkwardly across the street, his helmet's screen cracked in thunderbolt jags.

Eila leapt into the air and flapped furiously, putting distance between her and her assailants. The buildings surrounding her opened up, and she twisted and darted erratically to avoid the barrage of projectiles coming at her. After she flew over a building and out of sight of the Oathkeepers, she glanced back.

Freedom. She had escaped. She would be more careful next time. As she hovered, she wondered how they had found her, how they had been so silent in their approach. She placed a hand against her beating heart and took a deep breath.

A blue flash, and hot pain seared her hip. The projectile continued streaking toward the clouds as Eila looked down.

Three Oathkeepers came out of the roof's shadow beneath her. The first hint that she wasn't free was the hum of their wings as they took off. The second was their glowing palms as they summoned their magic.

"Shit," Eila mouthed. *When had they recruited faeries?* She fired a shard of ice at one of the fae's chests, but she darted to the side.

Vines conjured from thin air snaked toward Eila as though they had a will of their own. Eila had seen nature magic before, and she could combat it if she were fast enough. The vine wrapped tightly around her wrist, but Eila clenched her fist, then laid her other palm on the vine and froze it from the inside out, causing it to harden and turn black.

She flicked her wrist, and the brittle vine flew off.

Another bullet whizzed through the gap between her thighs. She turned to the fae who seemed to prefer technology to magic, but before she could subdue him, her first attacker regained her composure, hands glowing red as she conjured a ring of fire that glowed fiercely as it shot toward her.

Eila was outnumbered but would not give up. She conjured a blizzard before her, and the ice and snow turned to steam as the fiery ring hit them. Eila sent out snow until the three were forced to shield their vision from the onslaught.

Eila darted skyward. She flew fifty meters before the three Oathkeepers could look for their target. She hovered a hundred meters above them, hoping her black fatigues would blend with the night sky.

The fae formed a triangle. Eila wanted to dart away, but movement might draw their attention. The trigger-happy fae glanced at something on their wrist, a flashing red light that pulsed as he stretched out an arm. As he raised his arm, the light got brighter.

Eila's blood ran cold. *It tracks magic. When I use my power, they can find me. Shit!*

Trigger-happy stared up. Though Eila could not see his face, she could sense his triumph. As one, the Oathkeepers ascended.

Eila's palms pulsed white, and the light got so bright that the world turned blurred. She gasped, shielding her eyes. It was over almost as quickly as it had begun, but the afterburn stung her retinas. She tried to focus on the three targets below her.

No, not three. Four.

Five.

Six.

What the hell is happening?

A flash of green and blond appeared between the Oathkeepers, and two small humanoids the size of Gizmo who were made of fire danced around her enemies. The Oathkeepers turned toward the new arrivals, blinking away their confusion from the light blast as the green and blond flash flew at them, flaming hands outstretched.

Lyrian?

In all his blazing glory. Taking advantage of his stun blast, he punched the nearest Oathkeeper, whose head jerked sideways. The flames on his hands burned the fae's black clothing, and the fae stopped flapping his wings and dropped to the rooftop like a falling star.

Eila now realized that the two humanoids were elemental minions, created from Lyrian's magic to disrupt and stupefy. They orbited the other fae, teasing and blinding them. The Oathkeepers swatted at the distractions like they were annoying flies as Lyrian flew up to meet Eila.

Her breath caught at the determination in Lyrian's face, which she found attractive. His eyes blazed as he hovered beside her. "Are you okay?"

"What are you doing here?"

Lyrian faced Trigger-Happy as the Oathkeeper shot between them. "Not now. Not here. Want to finish this together?"

Eila grinned, and they dropped down to the remaining fae.

The Oathkeeper on the rooftop rolled to extinguish his flaming clothing.

"Frost and fire?" Lyrian smirked.

Eila nodded curtly. She concentrated on the left, and the air glowed white and red as a funnel of frozen air and snow flew out parallel to a column of flames. The Oathkeepers stopped swatting at the fire minions and rapidly descended to escape the attack.

They were too slow. Lyrian set his target's back on fire. Eila's target's wings froze and she plummeted, but her flaming companion caught her.

"Let's go," Eila stated.

Lyrian nodded, and they sped over the rooftops, Eila leading the way.

CHAPTER FIVE

Eila landed on the grass. Lyrian touched down a moment later.

"I'm tired of saving you," Lyrian quipped, smiling. "Mother, I've missed you." He reached out, but Eila stepped back, uncertain and confused.

"What in the Iron Wastes is going on, Lyrian?" Eila glanced around to ensure they were alone. She had landed beneath a stand of trees. The city was not in sight, and the canopy's shadow hid them from passersby. Under the Bridge was a short distance away.

"What do you mean?" Lyrian looked hurt. "I came to find you."

"At the exact moment that I was once again in trouble with Oathkeepers, as though you're bound to me and my pain?"

Lyrian produced a soothing smile, head cocked to the side as he stepped toward Eila. "I *am* bound to you, my love. From the moment I saw you, I was yours, and you were mine."

Eila shook her head. "I need answers."

Lyrian ran his fingers through his hair. "What's going on? I thought you'd be pleased to see me."

Eila's face set. "You *just happened* to find me when I ran into trouble?"

"When are you not in trouble?" Lyrian chuckled.

Eila tightened her jaw. "And you *just happened* to come to my aid in the jail?"

"I heard you were in trouble, and I wanted to return the enormous gift you gave me. One for which you were punished—"

"What were you doing standing in a Faerie Door talking to Maevis Blackwing?" Eila asked.

"Who?" Lyrian shot back.

Eila stepped toward Lyrian and beat her fists against his chest. "You're working for the enemy!" She could barely control herself. Faced with the person she had been mentally trying to defend for over a week, it all came pouring out. She had forced the idea that Lyrian could be on the side of wrong into a drawer in her mind, but it strained to escape. Eila realized she hoped it wasn't true, but she was unable to deny the evidence any longer. "It *was* you. You were after the Sceptre, and you took it. *That* was why you were caught in the palace. *That* was why you've been speaking to Maevis. It wasn't Silas. It was *you*."

Her emotions surged. She had never felt them this strongly, so she didn't understand what was happening. Even Lyrian, whose Summer kin were not as repressed as their Winter counterparts, was taken aback as he looked at Eila.

"Eila. Eila! Shhh…" Lyrian soothed, embracing her. She endured the wave of emotion as they stood there, two lovers in the shadows. He waited patiently until Eila peeled away. She wouldn't meet his eyes but stared at the grass, wiping the tears and composing herself.

"I'm sorry," she announced at last. "I don't know where all that came from."

Lyrian gave her a sympathetic glance. "You've been spending too much time in the human world. I haven't seen emotion like that in centuries, and never from a Winter fae." He studied her face, wondering where to begin. "You really believe I'm the enemy?"

"I don't know what to believe," Eila stated. "There's a lot happening that I can't explain, and you just appeared in the middle of the night when I'm under attack. That doesn't help."

Lyrian sighed. "Let's take this one issue at a time, okay?"

Eila met his green eyes. She did not see any deception in them.

"I came to find you tonight because I had news, and you deserved to hear it. I saw the light show you and the Oathkeepers were making in the sky, and I stepped in. It was a coincidence. I wasn't joking when I said you always seem to be in trouble here on Earth."

Eila looked skeptical.

"As for the prison, I told you there are people watching out for you on both sides of the door. I was sent to extract you, and I did."

"How did you know about the entrances, the tunnels, and the secret routes?" Eila asked. "It doesn't make sense."

"Intel." He was so close now. The scent of fresh-cut grass and daisies reached Eila's nostrils. "You think we'd undertake an operation like that without knowing what we were doing? You have a lot of allies, believe it or not, and I volunteered because of the debt I owed you for helping me escape."

Eila's lips thinned. Lyrian's head cocked to the side the way it always did when he was going to kiss her.

She backed up a step. "The Faerie Door and Maevis?"

Lyrian straightened, creases forming on his brow. "The only faerie doors I've used are the few that are publicly accessible. And this...Maevis?" He sighed. "I've been dealing with matters on the other side of the door. I haven't paid attention to what's happening here."

Eila studied his eyes. "I still don't know what to believe."

Lyrian's shoulders slumped. "Believe in our history, Eila." He brought his finger to her chin. "Believe what you know of me, and I of you." He guided her face toward his, and their lips met. The kiss was frosty at first, but his heat thawed Eila, and she fell into him. He broke the kiss and stared into her eyes. "Believe in *us*."

Eila held his gaze. She had to believe him since, when asked a direct question, fae had to tell the truth. Lyrian might not be telling her the full story, but she apparently had allies on the other side. He had not spoken to Maevis through the Faerie Door, and he *had* come to deliver news when he found Eila battling the Oathkeepers.

She went up on her toes and wrapped her arm around his neck. "I've missed you so much." She kissed him again, and their tongues played. The world fell away and she was back at the fete that summer eve, embracing Lyrian for the first time.

"I've missed you, too," Lyrian murmured when they broke the kiss. "More than I can tell you."

Eila licked her lips, closing her eyes to compose herself. "I hate to be the one to break this spell, but you said you had news."

Lyrian nodded. "I have, and it's not pretty."

"Uglier than being cried on by a hysterical faerie?" Eila hoped the quip would clear the air.

Lyrian smiled and pressed her hand to his chest. "It's the Winter Court. The worst has happened."

Fenris' words came back to her.

"Your land is dying," Lyrian continued. "Someone succeeded in stealing the Icicle Sceptre, and chaos has erupted across the realm. Queen Amara has tried to hide the matter, but news leaked to the other realms, and the destruction is spreading."

Eila's smile faded. "How bad is it?"

"Horrible. Everwinter is melting. Your people are struggling for food, and more requests come to my court each day for crops and resources. Our fields are withering too, and my people are panicking."

Eila frowned. "Why would the other realms be affected? I was told the Sceptre was tied to the Winter Court. Its influence shouldn't spread."

Eila shuddered. In her mind's eye, she saw water dripping as the palace slowly collapsed. She saw Winter fae emigrating as the realm melted into oblivion. She also saw a face with sharp features and platinum hair.

"Do they know who stole the Sceptre?" Eila gritted her teeth in anticipation of the response.

Lyrian's face darkened.

"Silas," Eila didn't need his confirmation. An owl gave a somber hoot.

"He hasn't been seen for a week, or so Aria tells me. Amara is trying to keep it quiet, but she can't."

Eila put her hands behind her back and took a deep breath as she strolled around and processed the information. How could things have crumbled so quickly? They might have kept the Oath of Realms from being broken, but the real bad guys were still out there.

Her heart thudded as she imagined Silas running through the Winter realm with his prize. Did he want total destruction so he could rebuild the realm to his liking, or was he trying to dethrone Queen Amara?

"I am not alone in this journey, and I will not sit solo on the throne. Once he has the Icicle Sceptre, the world will fall to our shadow and bow to our command. It is inevitable."

"Fuck." Eila stamped her foot on the ground. Her mind was filled with Silas' grinning face. He had turned the court against Lyrian and urged Eila's banishment. She had wondered why Silas was targeting her, but she couldn't understand why. Now she knew what he had sought. *"Fuck!"*

Lyrian folded his arms. "There's one more thing."

Eila met his gaze.

"It's…it's your father."

Eila's eyes widened.

"He's in the dungeon," Lyrian stated.

"Why?" Eila asked, fists clenching without her knowledge.

Lyrian chewed his lip. "According to Aria, the evidence suggests he was part of the plot. He's being held for conspiring against the court. I'm sorry."

Eila didn't know whether to laugh or cry. She knew little about her father, but she was sure of his loyalty. She couldn't believe he would participate in something so heinous and destructive, especially after how Eila's mother died to protect and defend the realm. He didn't have it in him. Whatever game Silas was playing, it was clever and dangerous.

She had to thwart it.

"Eila?"

"Hmmm?" Eila replied, lost in her thoughts.

"You've got that look in your eye."

"What look?"

Lyrian smirked. "That look that says you're ready to turn on the mischief."

She turned her stare to Lyrian, a grin appearing. "You shouldn't know that look yet."

"Oh, but I do. Whatever you need, just tell me. I'm with you, and we will make it happen."

The looks they exchanged were hot enough to ignite the trees. "I need to go back to Faerie. Banishment or not, I need to put a stop to all this."

CHAPTER SIX

Corvus stiffened when they stepped into Under the Bridge, eyes narrowing.

"Corvus—" Eila started.

"No." He puffed his chest out. "What the fuck is *he* doing here?"

"Easy." Lyrian held his hands out. "It's not what you think."

"Eila, move away from him," Corvus commanded, fingers flexing at his sides. The room dimmed.

"No, Corvus." Eila stepped in front of the Summer fae. "We have it all wrong. I promise we can trust him."

"Bullshit," Corvus ground out. "Grim told you what he saw."

"It's not like that." Eila approached her friend as the light continued to dim. "We've talked it through, and it wasn't Lyrian. It was Silas all along."

"Ha!" Corvus crowed. "*He* told you that, did he? Convenient. And what the hell is he doing here? Shouldn't he be frolicking in Faerie?"

Lyrian replied. "I came to warn Eila that the Winter Court is dying, and her father…"

"Shut the fuck up." Corvus turned his attention to Eila. "I want to hear it from you."

Eila frowned. She appreciated Corvus' concern, but she could make her own decisions. She didn't need a protector.

She spread her fingers, palms glowing white. "Calm down, Corvus. Let's talk this through. There's enough going on without having to deal with your insecurities. Will you listen, or do you want to fight?"

Corvus' gaze bored into Eila, but his shoulders softened. The room brightened. "Explain."

Lyrian took a breath.

"Not you." Disgust wreathed Corvus' features. "Eila."

Eila shared everything Lyrian had told her about the court, her father's capture, and the corruption destroying the realms. As she spoke, Corvus' skepticism was clear.

"We need to stop Silas. My father's freedom depends on it, as does my realm's survival."

Corvus gripped a nearby chair's back, knuckles white. "That's a hard turn from our discussion with Fenris." He took a long breath, still uncertain. "What do you propose to do?"

"I need to go back," Eila stated. "To find out what's going on so that we can stop this. I can't do that from London."

Corvus sighed. "I have to state the obvious."

Eila waited expectantly.

"You were banished," Corvus declared. "If the queen finds out you returned, they'll…" Pain flared in his eyes. "They'll punish you, Eila. Worst case, they'll execute you. You know how ruthless your people are."

Lyrian stepped out from behind Eila. "If I may be so bold as to speak…"

Corvus' eyes narrowed.

"The situation is dire," Lyrian continued, stopping beside Eila. "If we do nothing, the devastation could grow too bad to reverse. Few know the Winter Court and the palace as well as Eila does, so what choice do we have? Eila's exile will mean nothing if there's no Winter Court."

"With the greatest of respect," Corvus replied, little of it in his voice, "I'd rather direct my concerns to the one person in this room I trust."

Lyrian stepped forward, eyes flashing with anger. "And while you debate the moral quandaries of trusting someone who has saved Eila's life, and who continues to keep her best interests locked in his heart, her world is dying. Quite frankly, I don't give a shit what you think of me. I only care about Eila's opinion, and like it or not, she stands by my side on this matter. So, are you in?"

They glared at each other.

Corvus finally gave a curt nod. "I'd follow Eila into any darkness."

A rush of warmth rushed through as she gazed at Corvus.

Lyrian had softened at Corvus' words. "Then we work on a game plan."

"Agreed," Eila replied.

"Agreed," Corvus added. "Where do we start?"

They sat around one of Grimrock's tables, Lyrian beside Eila. Time passed quickly as they gathered and recapped their intel, working to figure out their next move. With Grimrock still gone, Eila was hesitant to proceed, but they needed to act since time wasn't on their side.

Corvus contributed where he could, despite his sparse knowledge about modern-day Faerie and particularly the Winter Court. They threw around ideas about how to reach out to Aria in secret, and paths to avoid detection by the very people who kicked Eila out of the court. The planning ground to a halt when they reached a vital point that none of them could find a solution to.

How were they going to find an unmanned Faerie Door to let them get to the Winter Court without detection?

"We need the lens," Corvus stated what they were all thinking. "It's the only way I can see to get in. Even then, we have no guarantee which doorway the lens will take us through, and what court we will arrive in." He looked at Lyrian. "Are there any unmonitored doorways to the Summer Court?"

Lyrian exchanged glances with Eila. Eila wondered if Lyrian could read the question in her mind. How had he known about the doors that had let her escape the Oathkeepers' jail? And were any of those doors a viable option?

"I only know about a few of the secret doors," Lyrian replied. "They all lead into and out of the Summer Court. I know of no doors that lead to the Winter Court."

"We need that mirror," Eila announced. "Corvus, have you seen it around? Grimrock had it last, right? Did he take it with him when he left?"

"I don't know," Corvus replied honestly. "If we knew where Grimrock went, maybe we'd have an answer, but we haven't heard from him in days." He asked the question that was on Eila's mind. "Do you think he's okay?"

Lyrian looked at them, then at the book Grimrock had left open on the desk. He idly flicked through the pages.

"I hope so," Corvus replied.

"Who is Grimrock?" Lyrian asked.

Eila described her troll friend, amused when Lyrian's eyes widened.

"A troll?" Lyrian asked. "No one has seen an elder troll for…"

"Centuries," Eila replied. "At least, not in Faerie."

She outlined Grimrock's interest in history and how he had been hiding here, archiving knowledge.

"He sounds like a great guy," Lyrian returned. "Shame we can't add him to our team. Someone like that would be invaluable to—"

A door slammed.

"Why can't I go with you?" Grimrock asked when he reached the bottom of the stairs.

Eila beamed. "Grimrock!" She ran toward the stone troll. He was a fierce sight, the hood of his long cape masking his face in shadow. She wrapped her arms around his unyielding flesh, ignoring the discomfort of hugging someone so rocky.

"Eila," Grimrock replied, gently placing a hand atop her head.

"Where the hell have you been, Balboa?" Corvus asked, smiling. "We were worried about you."

Grimrock stiffened when he saw Lyrian.

Eila stepped back to defuse the situation. She sighed, then muttered, "I've just had to explain to Corvus. Now I've gotta clear it with you, too." She explained, "It's okay, big guy. He's on our side."

Grimrock grunted, lip curling.

"Mother!" Lyrian exclaimed. "Is everyone in your cohort against me?"

"You're not helping," Eila replied.

Grimrock slowly walked toward Lyrian. He stopped a few feet away and bent his neck to gaze down at the faerie.

Eila impotently placed one hand on his stomach to hold him back. "Grim, I'm serious. Lyrian explained it all. It wasn't him you saw. It was Silas, or one of Silas' lackeys. Either way, he's on our side. He's going to help us. He came here to warn us and tell us what he knows."

Grimrock's nostrils flared as he lowered the hood.

Eila was afraid he would launch a fist at Lyrian's skull and squash it like a grape. "Grim, please! Faerie is in danger. We need to work together if we're going to save it."

Grimrock shifted, softening as he removed the cloak. He aimed his words at Lyrian. "Speak true. You promise that you will not harm Eila, and you are here to help us."

Eila stepped back, studying Lyrian's face. Grimrock was smart to ask a direct question she knew Lyrian could not lie in answer to. She bristled, breath catching.

"I will not harm Eila," Lyrian replied flatly. "I am here to help you."

Grimrock held his gaze a moment longer. "Then you joined at the perfect time. I have news that might lead to dire consequences."

"We've heard," Eila informed him, outlining what Fenris and Lyrian had shared.

"Then it is spreading," Grimrock stated.

"Where the hell have you been, anyway?" Eila asked. "We've been worried about you."

Grimrock turned to the books. As he spoke, he ran a finger over several volumes. "I made a pilgrimage to a forgotten place. An ancient place lost to time and memory that clings to this earth as a barnacle clings to the hull of a ship."

Eila raised her eyebrows. "Wow, remember that turn of phrase for your novel."

Lyrian looked confused.

"I'll tell you later," Eila whispered.

"The remaining intellectuals of my order maintain it," Grimrock continued. "I sought the answers to the riddle. The items and objects are linked, Eila. I just couldn't figure the connection or understand their importance."

Corvus tapped his fingers impatiently, irritated by Grimrock's slow speech. "But now you have? Just cut to the chase."

Grimrock faced Corvus. The ravenkin was taken aback by the troll's intensity. "It's not just the Sceptre. There's much more to it."

"More to what?" Eila asked, her impatience clear.

"The Sceptre wasn't the first domino," Grimrock replied, finally pulling a book off the shelves. He slammed it on the table beside the book Lyrian had been fiddling with and found the page he was after. It held the image of a green crystal radiating vines and flowers that coiled around the jewel. "That's the Verdant Crystal."

He swiftly moved back to the shelves and drew out another book. The next page showed a crown made of twigs and berries and acorns.

"That looks like Fenris' crown," Eila stated.

Corvus' brow creased.

Lyrian folded his arms, watching the troll rifle through books with interest.

Grimrock slammed another book down and opened it to a page that showed an amulet that resembled the sun hanging from a thin leather cord.

"The Sunfire Amulet," Grimrock declared. He turned the pages of the book Lyrian had leafed through. "The Icicle Sceptre."

Eila had never seen him like this before, so feverish and animated. "I don't understand."

"They're connected," Corvus chipped in, brow furrowed as he stared at the pages. His ravenkin tendencies would not let his gaze leave the page. He tapped the Verdant Crystal. "Spring." He tapped the Sunfire Amulet. "Summer." His gaze flicked to Lyrian, then to the crown. "Autumn."

Finally, he tapped the Sceptre, glancing at Eila. "Winter."

Eila examined the items. "Spring, Summer, Autumn, Winter… the four Faerie kingdoms."

Grimrock nodded solemnly.

"I still don't understand," Eila said. "Yes, the Icicle Sceptre was stolen, but how are the other items linked to the kingdoms?" She placed a finger on the Harvest Crown. "That is Fenris' crown, is it not? And the Autumn Court hasn't broken or fallen because the crown is outside of its jurisdiction."

"And the Amulet?" Eila turned to Lyrian. "You know the Summer Court. Have you heard of that item?"

"Of course," Lyrian replied. "It is given to the Summer Court's champion. It provides the kingdom with energy and power."

"Is it still with the champion?" Corvus snarled.

"The last I checked, it was," Lyrian replied. "I've heard no rumors about the item going missing."

"That leaves the crystal," Eila declared. "Where is that?"

Grimrock replied. "The troll elders informed me that the item was kept in a sacred grove within the Autumn Court, guarded by dryads."

"I don't like that word," Corvus stated.

"What word?" Eila asked.

"'Should,'" Corvus replied.

Grimrock sighed. "The dryads were found dead yesterday morning, and the crystal was gone. No one has information about who entered or how that occurred."

"I have a bad feeling about this," Eila muttered.

Grimrock lowered his head. "It gets worse."

"Of course it does," Corvus added.

The troll continued. "In the temple I visited, I saw a scripture that speaks of a ritual that uses the focal items from the four faerie courts to unlock a second Cataclysm."

"It always comes back to the fucking Cataclysm." Corvus shook his head. "Like it wasn't bad enough the last time."

Eila turned to Grimrock. "What does the ritual involve?"

"It must take place on one of the power spots in the faerie realms, locations that are sacred and thrum with ancient magical energy." Grimrock stood taller. "It is called 'the Frostfire Convergence.'"

The room fell silent.

"The Frostfire Convergence." Eila tested the name on her lips. "I've never heard of it." She looked at Lyrian. "Have you?"

"I have," Lyrian replied sadly. "That legend is passed down through my family. People all over my land fear it."

Eila turned back to Grimrock. "What do we do? You've read the texts, so you know the ritual. What do we need to do to stop it?"

Grimrock glanced at Lyrian. "It is said that the ritual can only be successful when all the items are combined and the final ingredient is present."

"Ingredient?" Corvus asked.

"We are standing on a precipice," Grimrock stated. "The Sceptre was taken. The Crystal was stolen. It is clear that someone seeks to unite the four items, so we must locate the Sunfire Amulet and protect the Crown." He paused.

"Say it," Eila urged. "Say what you're holding back."

"There is a final item," Grimrock offered. "One I believe we must pursue if we are to prevent another Cataclysm. If we prevent our enemies from obtaining it, it should cause them to fail in their quest."

The troll picked up his cloak, reached into a pocket, and drew out a scroll, its edges dried and cracked. He unrolled it on the table to reveal a faded illustration of an altar glowing from within. Surrounding the alter were flames, though Eila couldn't see the source. There was writing in an unknown script.

"What does it say?" Eila asked.

Grimrock tapped the altar. "That is the final ingredient. The catalyst to complete the ritual. That is the 'Heart of Frostfire.'"

"Why is it surrounded by flames?" Corvus asked.

The Summer Fae adjusted his collar, and a thin leather cord was briefly visible.

"The artifact is guarded," Eila stated as an ancient tale whispered in the back of her mind. "Isn't it, Grim?"

Grimrock nodded. "To stop the Convergence, we'll have to fight an evil so ancient that it is almost forgotten."

Eila straightened, catching Lyrian's and Corvus' gazes. Her stomach knotted as she struggled to process the gravity of the situation.

This morning, I was baking brownies. Now it's down to this merry band of warriors to save the world.

CHAPTER SEVEN

"There's only one doorway that I know of that remains unguarded," Eila offered as she, Grimrock, Corvus, and Lyrian walked quickly along a busy London street. Morning had arrived. The sky was filled with gray clouds that threatened a downpour. Men and women in suits and coats bustled along the streets, and the roads were choked.

Eila, Lyrian, and Corvus blended into the crowd. Passing men marveled at Eila's face, form, and bright hair. Lyrian drew female gazes as he passed.

Grimrock towered over the crowd, standing out like a sore thumb. Several times, he had to duck or hunch over to avoid drawing excess attention.

Eila led the way, utilizing what she had learned of London's streets to find her way to the location she knew held the doorway back to her past. The urge to fly was great, but since only three of their company could do so, they were grounded by the troll.

They all ducked as a troop of Oathkeepers wove through the traffic on motorcycles that rumbled and roared. Eila flashed back to her rooftop fight and the short time she had spent in their jail. This was not a good time to be captured.

After an hour of trekking through London's heart, the streets quieted down. The tall buildings made way for modest ones, and Eila saw overpasses and motorways stretching before her like twisted spaghetti.

She scanned for the familiar as she retraced the path that led her into London all those nights ago. It seemed like a distant memory.

Beneath one underpass, she saw them—a huddle of homeless people sitting around the flaming oil drum. One stood out to her, looking vibrant in a coat that had once been pristine white but was now stained and muddy.

Grub was eating something Eila couldn't see.

"This way." She maintained a distance between her party and the oil drum. When they stood beneath the underpass, a familiar stale scent met Eila's nostrils. Her heart hammered as she thought back to being summoned into Queen Amara's throne room and the physical force that had rocked her when she had been informed of her banishment.

I shouldn't go back. I was banished. Queen Amara will find me. She'll know I've returned. I'll be executed. My father will be humiliated.

Wasn't her father in prison now under false pretenses?

Eila's mind explored the "what ifs?" She stared at the spot where the Faerie Door opened.

Grimrock drew out the lens and studied its glowing jewels. "We're here."

Eila nodded. "We are."

"Are you ready to do this?" Lyrian asked, placing a hand on the small of Eila's back.

Corvus glared at the back of his head. "I'll ask one more time. Are we sure we don't want to bring Fenris in on this?"

They had had that conversation multiple times. On the one hand, Fenris had powers beyond Eila's comprehension. He was a useful ally, and he was already sniffing out ways to protect the realms and stop the madness.

On the other hand, he possessed the Harvest Crown. By bringing him along, they'd jeopardize the item. Eila had reasoned it was better to leave him in the dark so no one would know about Nemora, the crown, or Fenris' location. That was the best way to keep it safe.

"We're sure. Let's do this," Eila replied.

Grimrock stood in the spot where the lens glowed brightest. Holding up a hand, he muttered words in an ancient tongue Eila didn't understand, moving his hands in a circular pattern. The air before him rippled and sparked, and then purple magic flashed from a single point. The Faerie Door stood before them, warbling and waiting to accept entrants.

"We're doing this?" Eila asked, turning to Lyrian and then to Corvus.

"We are," Lyrian replied.

Eila took a deep breath. Part of her believed the queen's influence might block her return to the Winter Court. As she strode through the door, the Nether calling her, she thought about the last time she had entered into Faerie, when a corrupt fae had been attempting to break the Oath of Realms.

Power rushed around her, the maelstrom now a friend. Lowering her head, she strode through the passage between realms, and finally stepped across the threshold of the door into Faerie.

A blast of wintry air met her skin, and snow struck her face. The sentinel rocks stood around her like ancient guardians. She spread her arms and beamed. The scent of the pine trees was a welcome delight. Eila realized how much she had missed the frozen tundra and the white blankets of clouds and snow covering the land and sky.

"Welcome home," Lyrian announced, drawing up beside Eila. Although he was thinly clad, he seemed unaffected by the cold. His skin glowed as he used his powers to send heat through his body.

"Oh, Mother," Corvus called, joining Eila's other side. Even in his thick black jacket, he shivered, drawing his arms around his body to hold in the warmth. "They're not kidding when they talk about you guys being a frosty bunch."

Eila chuckled sympathetically. While breaking her banishment to serve the greater good was a big step, she wasn't the only one breaking the rules. Corvus and Grimrock had shared the banishment of Corvus' ancestors, as well as the details of his curse.

With chattering teeth, Corvus caught Eila's gaze. Eila's heart fluttered with appreciation at the loyalty and strength her friend showed.

"How come you aren't freezing your tits off?" Corvus asked Lyrian, looking at him with something akin to jealousy.

"Summer Court," Lyrian replied without further explanation.

Eila tilted her head toward Corvus. "You got any spare heat to help him?"

Lyrian met Eila's gaze and rolled his eyes. "Here."

He placed a hand on Corvus' shoulder.

Corvus flinched.

Lyrian's hand glowed orange, and his power spread over Corvus' shoulder and through his body until his glow rivaled Lyrian's.

Corvus relaxed, taking a long breath as sweat broke out on his brow. He muttered, "Thanks."

"How about you, big guy?" Eila asked when Grimrock emerged. "Do you need some heat to fight the chill?"

Grimrock shook his head. Not for the first time, Eila wondered about his biology, curious as to how temperature, pain, and sensation affected the troll's body.

Grimrock studied their surroundings. "I wondered whether the day I would return to the Winter Court would ever come."

"It's...pretty," Corvus stated. Due to the snow, visibility was limited. They could see only the tops of surrounding trees and an uneven, forgotten path that disappeared into the snow as it led down the mountain.

"It's better than the welcome I got in London." Eila started down. "It doesn't stink of shit here. No homeless people to speak of, either."

"Speaking ill of the homeless?" Corvus asked, speeding up to catch Eila as Lyrian stepped to her side.

Eila shrugged. "It's not the homeless I have a problem with. It's the signs of a broken economic system in which you guys don't look after your people. There shouldn't be homeless people if England is as prosperous as Jim says it is."

"Pay no attention to him," Corvus replied. "That dude is cuckoo for Coco Puffs."

Eila kept working her way down. "He might have a point. Don't you think so, Grim?"

Grim stomped behind them, dogged determination on his face. "I don't keep up with human politics."

"Probably for the best," Lyrian chimed in.

"Where are we going?" Corvus asked, shooting an irritated glance at Lyrian.

"To get the Heart," Lyrian answered as if it was obvious. He leaned close to Eila. "I thought ravens were one of the smart birds."

Eila couldn't help but grin.

"What did he say?" Corvus piped up. "Lyrian, you got something to say, say it to my face."

Lyrian smirked and continued walking.

"The Heart of Frostfire dwells within the everwinter in the outlands," Grimrock contributed. "A place few faeries go since the ground is so cold that no crops will grow. It is to the Frostfang's Cavern we tread."

"You know the way?" Corvus asked Eila.

She glanced at Grimrock. "I know someone who does."

"Who?" Corvus pressed.

Eila exchanged glances with Lyrian. "A mutual friend."

They made slow progress down the mountain. Eila wished she could just fly, but not with Grimrock in tow. Even with their combined strength, they could not lift him above the treetops.

The path was uneven and buried in snow in some places. Trusting her sense of direction, Eila led. The group was silent as they trod, the grim realization of what they were working toward lying heavy on them.

Strange things took place around them. Occasionally, the thick clouds parted, revealing a blackness in which purple electricity danced and pulsed.

The wildlife acted oddly as well. Mooncalves and deer sprinted away from unseen dangers several times. When that happened, the four prepared to fight, but nothing threatened them.

"That is not a good sign," Eila commented as stopped on a ledge beside a solberry tree. Its branches bore a thick blanket of snow, and the berries, which should have been gleamed gold, were black and gray. Eila plucked one, and the berry crumbled to dust in her hands. "It's true. The world is dying."

She looked down the cliff and saw a large body of water with a frozen surface. Hundreds of small black shapes littered the ice, some poking out, forever stilled.

"Freshwater silvertang," Lyrian commented. "All dead."

Corvus stopped beside them. "Could it not just be because it's so cold that the water froze before they could escape?"

Lyrian looked dubious. "You don't think the species evolved to survive in these lands? Silvertang are known for their hardiness, able to survive even the harshest winters in the Winter Court's lands."

"Clearly not those," Corvus remarked, wrapping his arms around himself, though he still glowed.

They walked for several hours, taking only one more short

break. Grimrock was carrying the pack, and he placed it on the ground. They sat on fallen logs to eat.

The blizzard had eased, leaving fresh powder in its wake. Ahead, the rolling hills vanished into white and blue. A bird's shriek reached their ears.

"Which direction?" Lyrian asked.

Eila peered forward. It was almost impossible to get her bearings since she could not see the sun. She remembered the flight weeks ago, then nodded ahead. "Straight on."

"How far is the cavern?" Corvus asked.

Eila shrugged. "As the raven flies? About two days, if Grimrock's books are accurate."

Corvus smiled, touched by Eila's shift from "crow" to "raven" in her directions. "And as the troll walks?"

Eila chewed her lip. "A lot longer." She glanced at Grimrock. "We have to move faster. If I'm right about where we are, we might be able to do something about that in a few miles."

"You also need to adjust your compass," Grimrock added. "West is in that direction."

"How do you know?" Corvus asked.

Grimrock closed his eyes and slowly rotated, then stopped. "Trolls always know the direction. We cannot get lost. Why do you think we make such good guardians?"

Eila grinned at Grimrock, impressed, then stared at where the landscape and the sky merged. She took a long breath. Another pulse of purple lightning darted above, and she felt as though a thousand eyes were watching them.

She thought about Queen Amara in her frozen palace and hoped she didn't have an inkling that Eila had returned. As brave as she was, she feared the queen's wrath.

CHAPTER EIGHT

"Over there," Corvus announced, eyes locked to the horizon. "Look."

Five black shapes were flying toward their group in formation.

"Shit! Scouts," Eila hissed. "Quick, hide."

They darted off the track, Lyrian, Corvus, and Eila found cover behind some large boulders that had tumbled off the mountain. As Eila settled behind a rock that was twice her size and four times her width, she realized that Grimrock hadn't followed the others.

Where was he?

She glanced at the place they had been standing and saw a solitary boulder on the path with fabric flapping at its sides. Grimrock was using his stone body as his disguise.

Eila grinned at Corvus, who gave the troll an appreciative nod. She couldn't see Lyrian.

The scouts silently flew toward the mountain and curved away from the group before disappearing into the clouds.

"They know," Lyrian stated, appearing at Eila's side.

"How?" Corvus asked.

Lyrian replied, "My best guess is the queen. She must be linked to the magic of this realm, able to detect surges and door use."

"You think?" Eila returned. She had never heard that, but she wouldn't put it past Queen Amara. The Winter Court's monarch was full of tricks, having ruled the realm for almost a millennium.

Lyrian shrugged. "I wouldn't be surprised."

They waited for a little longer before leaving their cover. As they approached the path, Grimrock unfurled.

"Remind me never to play hide and seek with you," Eila quipped.

Grimrock produced a smile.

Awareness heightened, they continued the trek, remaining close to features behind or under which they could hide if needed. After a mile or so, the group reached a stretch of flat and barren fields and the ghostly silhouette of a village.

"Civilization," Corvus offered.

"It's a start," Eila added. Although it was unlikely that the faeries who lived out here would know who Eila was or what her crimes had been, she had broken the terms of her banishment, and she was back among her people.

"Are you okay?" Corvus asked, sensing Eila's hesitation.

Lyrian wrapped an arm around Eila's waist. "You'll be fine. We've got you."

Corvus frowned.

Eila lifted her chin. "We can't stop. Let's go before the blizzard returns and Grimrock gets frozen to the spot."

Eila led the way again. Lyrian cast a cursory glance at Corvus before following her. Corvus paused, and Grimrock came up beside him.

"You have feelings for Eila," Grimrock stated flatly, peering at the village.

Corvus bristled. "Excuse me? No." His cheeks turned red as he fussed with his hair, shaking out the snow. "What's wrong with you?"

Grimrock just nodded and walked on.

Corvus glared at the back of the troll's head, then at Eila, and his shoulders relaxed. He lowered his head, then followed.

There were no lights on when they arrived at the village. They scanned the windows and the doors to see if any light leaked through but saw none. Although the cloud cover made it difficult to determine the time, Eila thought it was midday.

"Where is everyone?" she asked as they walked down the empty streets. The modest houses wood houses' doors had rounded tops. Some houses had flowerbeds in front, and others had window boxes that might once have been filled with blooms. Nearby was a small bare park with a frozen pond, fish frozen on the surface.

"I don't understand." Eila had worried about being detected, but now she was worried about a greater evil. What had driven everyone from the village? What was she missing?

Something creaked, and Eila turned sharply. Corvus was tentatively opening the door of a nearby home.

"What are you doing?" Eila hissed.

Corvus nodded for them to follow.

Eila looked at Lyrian and Grimrock for help. Lyrian shrugged. Grimrock gave nothing away. She rolled her eyes and followed Corvus into the house.

It had been abandoned. Someone had recently lived here, given a plate that hadn't been washed but had not accumulated mold or fungus. They explored the house, seeking clues as to where its residents had gone.

No letters or declarations. No messages or notes.

"They just vanished," Eila told the cold room. Her breath was a mist as she stared at an unmade bed and clothes on the floor.

"Any guesses?" Corvus asked, shivering as Lyrian's magic dwindled.

"Nothing I want to share yet." Eila's lips thinned.

Grimrock had patiently waited outside, watching the sky. Purple magic occasionally pulsed, sending jagged bolts through the gaps in the clouds. The snow had lessened, but given the mounds that had accumulated on Grimrock's shoulders and head, he hadn't moved since Corvus and Eila entered the house. Lyrian had wandered off.

"Anything?" Grimrock asked, peeling his eyes off the clouds.

"None," Corvus returned. "It's as though everyone just vanished. *Poof!*"

"That's not possible," the troll replied.

"Nor is it true," Eila added. "Might have been a mass exodus. The outer villages have it the hardest, so if the crops die, they're likely to move closer to the palace."

"Is that what you believe has happened?" Grimrock asked.

Corvus watched her closely.

"No," Eila confessed. Then, "Where's Lyrian?"

"Here," Lyrian announced, coming around the corner from a side street. "I wanted to check the rest of the town to see what's what."

"And?" Eila asked.

Lyrian lifted his chin. "Turns out, we're not alone."

CHAPTER NINE

There was a solitary light flickering in a house at the edge of the village.

Lyrian led the way, staying silent as they drew closer. The house was larger than most, and more worn. Its timber beams were crooked and splintering, the roof bowing beneath the weight of the snow. A candle illuminated a window on the upper floor, sending dancing shadows over the walls.

"I couldn't see who is inside," Lyrian whispered.

Eila walked up to the door and raised her fist. She hesitated before knocking, the noise like gunshots in the quiet village.

No response.

"Again," Corvus encouraged, gaze locked on the window.

Eila knocked again. Still no answer. She reached for the knob and opened the door slowly. The resulting creak sounded like the bellow of an animal in pain.

Before she stepped inside, a light blinded her, followed by a blast of cold wind. Something pulled on Eila's ankles, and she nearly toppled. A thick sheet of ice encapsulated her ankles, anchoring them to the ground. The others gasped when sheets of ice also rooted them to the spot.

Fluttering wings drew their attention to the upper window as a shape emerged from it. Eila couldn't see the faerie behind the blast of magic that rained down on her, sending shards of ice down over their heads.

Eila created a block of ice above her to keep from being hit. Lyrian's Summer heat pulsed, melting the shards before they could do any damage.

"Hold!" Eila called. "We're not your enemies."

"You're not friends!" the faerie called back, landing nearby with a thud. She held up her hands, eyes darting over the company.

Eila quelled her magic, and the block cracked and fell to the ground. She shrugged pieces off her shoulders as she tried to face the faerie despite her ankles being locked in place.

The faerie had deep lines on her face. Her thick hair was tied back in a bunch, and the hunch in her back revealed her years. Despite her appearance, her eyes were keen as she glanced at the four.

"Friends don't trespass," the faerie croaked. "If'n you knock and nobody answers, you take the hint and go away. That was what they all did. Left, I tell you. Abandoned their homes, and for what? Leaving enough food and shelter for old Agnes to thrive, that's what."

Her heavy brows rose. "You're a strange bunch, ain't ya? Marauders come to take the last of the stock? Well, you ain't having it as long as I draw breath!"

She screeched the last words, throwing her hands forward to release a cyclone of swirling white powder. The air twist tore toward Grimrock, who held his ground. The power blew his cloak back but did not otherwise affect him.

Lyrian sent flaming balls toward Agnes. They lit up the street before finding their target.

Agnes held up her arms and conjured an ice shield. Water trickled down Agne's chest as the final ball reached her. Eila sent a blast of snow and ice at the ball, knocking it off-course. It hit the ground and fizzled out.

"*No, Lyrian!*" Eila shouted. "*She is not the enemy.*"

"She attacked us!" Lyrian exclaimed.

"Agnes," Eila placated. "Please. Trust one of your kin. We are here because we need help."

Agnes laughed. "Help? There's none here. The world is changing, and we must weather the storm. Help abandoned this village and flocked to the palace this morning. It's every faerie for themselves in this lawless land."

While Agnes was talking, Eila directed her power at her feet. She sent small cracks through the ice until she could turn to the ancient fae.

"We have the answer," Eila returned, earning a cocked eyebrow from Corvus. "We can help."

"You're talking nonsense," Agnes shot back, softening her stance only slightly. "But if you want to parley, let's get it over with so I can send you on your way."

"Great." Eila watched her carefully. "Set them free, and we can move this along."

"No." Agnes looked down her nose at the others. "They stay outside. You and I will parley. I'm not talking with no Summer Court fae and his mongrels."

Lyrian's lips thinned. Corvus' brows furrowed. Grimrock remained still.

Eila sighed. "Very well."

With a snap of Agnes' fingers, the ice around the ankles of the rest of the party dissipated. She turned and entered her home, leaving the door ajar for Eila.

Corvus rushed over to Eila. "You're not going in there alone, are you?"

Eila guided Corvus away from the house. "These are my people. You don't understand their ways. She won't talk unless it's just us. Wait outside. I'll be fine."

Corvus gave her a doubtful look. Lyrian shifted uneasily.

Eila entered the house, closing the door behind her.

Corvus shivered, the cold settling in with each flake of snow. He folded his arms, eyes locked on the downstairs window, ready to defend Eila.

"Goddammit, how do faeries live in this weather?" he asked Grimrock, teeth chattering.

He didn't know what was up with the big guy, but he hadn't acted normal since they'd stepped through the portal. He had an intensity Corvus hadn't seen before. He was concentrating, rather than displaying the studious and whimsical nature Corvus had come to appreciate.

Grimrock shifted. "We adapt to our surroundings. This is where they live."

Corvus found it impossible to imagine growing up somewhere as cold as this.

"It is also a defense mechanism," Grimrock added. "It is hard for enemies to conquer when they cannot endure the elements."

"You're telling me." Corvus glanced at his hands. His fingertips were turning blue. "Hey, hot spring, mind giving me a top-up? I'm gonna get frostbite."

Lyrian glanced at Corvus and turned away without a word.

"Now that your girlfriend isn't watching, you can't be bothered to help?" Corvus growled.

Lyrian took a long breath. "Why would I help someone who doubts my intentions and continues to make things difficult?"

Corvus tucked his fingers into his armpits. "You know why. I'm trying on a new way of thinking, but you know how it goes. You can't teach an old dog new tricks."

"Eila says you're a bird."

"A raven," Corvus returned, oddly happy that Eila had spoken to Lyrian about him.

"So, go build a nest somewhere," Lyrian shot back. "Isn't that what birds do?"

"They fly south for the winter," Corvus replied, his irritation growing as he shivered. He hopped up and down, the heat spell all but gone.

Grimrock glanced at Corvus. "Ravens do not migrate."

Corvus rolled his eyes. "He said 'birds,' not 'ravens.'"

"My point stands," Grimrock replied, turning his gaze back to the house. "Not all birds migrate. Just swans, geese, and other waterfowl. Also swallows…"

"All right, all right." Corvus tried to take a deep breath, but the cold hurt his lungs. "The point is, I'm cold. Lyrian, do me a favor?"

Lyrian stared at the house.

"And you wonder why I don't trust you," Corvus muttered under his breath. His breath was a cloud, and his fingers, toes, elbows, and knees hurt. He could shout for Eila, but he didn't want to give Lyrian the satisfaction.

Corvus took a painful step toward Lyrian to offer a reluctant apology, but as he blinked, Lyrian and Grimrock disappeared.

Corvus reached out, arms as heavy as lead. He turned around, wind gusting around him, howling in his ears. Snow whipped up, and the houses of the village disappeared. He flinched, stomach lurching as the roar of a huge monster assaulted his eardrums. He searched the sky since he heard wingbeats but was unable to see the source until a column of blue light appeared.

He was on a ridge like a spine. Ahead of him, two people faced each other, shouting words he could not understand. One of the combatants was obscured by snow, but he recognized the other.

"Eila!" Corvus exclaimed.

Eila Snowshadow roared as she thrust her hands toward her enemy. A column of frozen blue light raced toward the other person. Searing red fire came at her, and the magic met in the middle. A flash from above showed him a frightful creature, all teeth and wings and blazing eyes.

Eila screamed in pain, the sound a dagger in Corvus' heart. An explosion sent the combatants reeling.

"*Eila!*" Corvus shouted, sprinting over to reach her. "*No!*" It was no use. As he ran, the scene receded, as though the tableau was powered by his steps. He ran until he was exhausted, then fell into the snow. The powder buried him where he lay, frost and ice settling into his bones.

"Hey, buddy. Wake up!"

A sharp pain flared on Corvus' cheek. When his eyes shot open, Grimrock was staring down at him.

Lyrian slapped his cheek, palms glowing.

"Warm him," Grimrock commanded.

"I am," Lyrian returned, sounding panicked. He placed his hands on Corvus' chest and sent heat through the ravenkin's body. Corvus' heart raced as he remembered his snowy burial. "Corvus? Are you okay?"

Corvus' teeth chattered long after the heat penetrated his body. Around him, the snow melted, leaving a deep imprint as he slowly pulled himself into a seated position. Grimrock helped him by placing a hand on the small of his back. "Take it easy, Corvus. Let it pass."

"What happened?" Lyrian asked.

Grimrock's eyes flashed. "Two things. One, you failed him."

Lyrian held up his hands. "Nobody told me I had to be a fae radiator when we stepped through that door."

"Kindness would—" Grimrock began.

"I didn't realize it would happen so fast!" Lyrian raked his fingers through his damp hair. "I was only making a point." He looked at Grimrock. "And the second thing?"

Grimrock's nostrils flared. "Corvus had a vision."

"A vision?" Lyrian asked, impressed. "What vision?"

The troll ignored Lyrian. "What did you see?"

The vision that had felt so real was melting away like the snow around Corvus. The edges were fuzzy. "The mountain again. Blazing blue and red magic at a crossroad. A winged monster that breathed fire. I also saw *her*, Grim. Eila..."

"Go on," Grimrock urged when the ravenkin didn't continue speaking.

Tear welled in Corvus' eyes. "I-I watched her die."

CHAPTER TEN

"You're going to get a cold ass sitting there like that," Eila announced as she stepped out of the house to find Lyrian and Grimrock crowded around Corvus. She frowned. "What happened?"

Lyrian helped Corvus to his feet. "My heat wore off and he got chilly. He's sorted now, aren't you, friend?"

Corvus frowned. "Yeah, sorted."

Eila looked at them curiously. "Ooookay. Well, do you want the good news or the bad news?"

"The good news," Lyrian requested as Agnes appeared behind Eila. The crone shifted past Eila to walk down the path.

"The good news is, Agnes will provide transportation." Eila beamed. "We can pick up the pace."

"That's amazing," Lyrian replied, rushing to Eila and embracing her.

"What's the bad news?" Corvus asked, hands in his pockets as he shuffled closer.

"I owe Agnes an unbreakable favor," Eila replied quietly enough that Agnes couldn't hear.

Lyrian sighed. "No. You didn't have to—"

"Yes, I did," Eila replied. "We needed transportation. We can't cross these lands at Grimrock's speed. We need the help."

"What's an unbreakable favor?" Corvus asked.

Lyrian frowned. "Are you that ignorant of fae culture?"

Eila put a hand on Lyrian's shoulder as Corvus bristled.

"An unbreakable favor is exactly what it sounds like," Grimrock explained. "Eila is obliged to provide whatever she asks for, no matter the size or magnitude."

Corvus' eyebrows rose. "Oh."

Eila frowned. "Keep an eye on the Winter Gazette in the coming weeks. Whoever Agnes puts the hit out on, I have to destroy without question." Although there was mirth in her reply, her three companions still looked somber. "Seriously, what in the Iron Wastes happened while I was in there?"

"Just cold." Corvus shrugged.

Animals grunted, drawing everyone's attention before Eila could reply. The smells of musk and dung reached her nostrils, and two creatures emerged out of the gloom that put Grimrock's stature to shame.

The majestic snowstriders were as muscular as deer and covered in a dense blanket of white fur. Thick antlers stretched to either side, almost as wide as they were long. Their hooves provided a solid foundation on which to traverse the wintry tundra. Their eyes were like jewels in their white faces, intelligence glinting in their pupils as they approached.

"Holy…" Corvus began, staring up at the creatures.

Eila beamed as the snowstriders stopped, air huffing from their nostrils that formed clouds before them. Leather harnesses encircled their chests and necks, the trailing straps leading to a cart with runners rather than wheels. Agnes shuffled out from behind the snowstriders, looking even smaller against their bulk.

Eila exclaimed, "I thought that you were kidding when you said you had snowstriders!"

"'Snowstriders?'" Corvus repeated.

Eila walked slowly around the creatures and ran a hand through one's coat. It leaned into the adoration. "Beautiful, aren't they? I've never seen one before. I thought they were legends, or they'd been lost to time. Aria was certain they'd been hunted to extinction." She shook her head in disbelief as the closest snowstrider nuzzled her. "If she could see this!"

"You're partly correct," Grimrock contributed.

Eila faced him.

"In the human realm, they speak of a man named Santa Claus, or 'Kris Kringle,' a jolly, rotund man who lives at the North Pole, and drives a sleigh with eight magical reindeer to deliver presents to every household on the 24th of December. Many humans don't know the folk tale originated in Faerie.

"When humans were trafficked into this realm, they worked with these creatures in the fields. When the Oath of Realms took effect, their stories twisted into myths of magical beings riding in sleighs pulled by reindeer. The origin was lost, but these creatures live on."

Grimrock strode over to the beasts. They bristled at his approach, unused to being approached by a creature almost as large as they were. He held a hand out toward the second snowstrider's cheek while staring into its jewellike eyes. "A being from the old world. A marvelous entity indeed."

Eila watched Grimrock, wondering about his past. His expression was sentimental as he brought up memories. Questions arose about his connection with these creatures and his time in the faerie realm, but she thought better of asking. The urgency of their mission triumphed over her curiosity. There would be time for questions when the threat of doom was gone.

"Nine," Corvus announced, surprising Eila from her reverie.

"Huh?" Eila asked.

Corvus held up his fingers he'd been busy counting on. "Nine. There were nine reindeer. Not eight."

The troll shook his head.

Corvus continued, lowering a finger as he spoke a name. "Dasher, Dancer, Prancer, Vixen, Comet, Cupid, Donner…"

"Blitzen," Grimrock added.

"Thanks." Corvus lowered his hands. "And Rudolph."

Grimrock sighed. "Rudolph was a contemporary addition, not in the original canon." He faced Corvus, keeping his hand on the snowstrider's cheek. "He was created in the thirties for marketing purposes. I do not count him."

"It doesn't matter when he was created. He's part of the *modern* canon. By your logic, none of the reindeer count since they were all fictional too."

Grimrock looked impressed and irritated.

"Yeah, Grim," Eila replied mischievously. "Fictional representations change. Otherwise, aren't we doomed to become what folklore dictates we are?" Eila remembered a conversation with the troll about his annoyance with the representation of his species in modern fiction.

For the first time since they arrived in Faerie, Grimrock laughed. The sound was like boulders crushed by a machine. "Fine. I accept your premise and stand corrected. *Nine* reindeer stemmed from the majesty of these creatures." He turned his attention back to the snowstrider. "It's not a surprise. What are your names, I wonder?"

Agnes piped up, irritated and bored. "The male is Blizzard, and the female is Glisten."

Eila smiled. "Blizzard and Glisten. Perfect names for perfect beings."

Agnes grabbed the reins and handed them to Eila. "They are obedient. Direct them with your intention, and they will obey your commands." Her gaze flashed to the others. "As long as you're of the Winter realm."

Eila smirked. "Sorry, boys. Looks like I'm driving."

"They will forage for food," Agnes added. "And they will tell you when they tire. Give them what they need, and they will meet your requirements. Any questions?"

Eila shook her head. "I will take care of them as if they are my own."

Agnes looked doubtfully at Eila. "Be certain you do. And remember…"

"I know," Eila replied. "I owe you."

"Hmmm." A croak rumbled through Agnes' throat as she returned to her front door. "Very well. Be on your way."

Eila motioned to the others. "Seats, gentleman. Let's get this show on the road."

Grimrock and Corvus boarded the cart. It swayed as the troll boarded. Corvus looked tiny sitting next to the troll.

Lyrian remained on the ground. "You're ready for this, Eila?"

"I am." Eila planted a kiss on Lyrian's lips, and the Summer Fae smiled. He went to board the sleigh, but Eila held him back. "Not you."

"What do you mean?" Lyrian asked. "I'm coming with you."

"Not yet." Shielding herself from the view of the others as she lowered her voice. "I need you to do me a favor first."

"I don't owe you an unbreakable one," Lyrian quipped. "What is it?"

"Contact Aria," Eila stated. "I want her to know what we're doing. Find her and tell her the full story. Please."

Lyrian frowned. "I don't understand."

Eila sighed. "We left without telling the others. The last Aria knows is from a letter I sent her via Fenris' people. Aria might look for me in the wrong places, and I want her to know the truth."

"Isn't that dangerous?" Lyrian asked. "The more people who know, the more who can stop you."

Eila shook her head. "I trust Aria. Not only that, but she is also connected with my father. If something goes wrong, we'll need backup. I need people to know what to do and how to stop this." She pressed her forehead against Lyrian's. "I'm not blind to the dangers on this mission. I need to know that should we fail, our efforts will not have been in vain."

Lyrian looked set to argue but gave a firm nod. "I'll find Aria. Then I'll fly back to you as fast as my wings can carry me."

"Thank you." Eila kissed him again, a tear sliding down her cheek.

Lyrian turned to leave. "I hope I avoid detection from the Winter Court security detail." He smirked. "I know my way out of your prisons now, though."

Eila chuckled, aware of the others watching her. "You're welcome. After you deliver the message and my task is complete, I'll meet you in the place Aria knows."

"Cryptic." Lyrian kissed Eila again. "May the Mother bless your passage."

Lyrian's wings beat furiously, and he shot off.

Eila joined Grimrock and Corvus on the cart, taking the driver's seat. "And then there were three."

"Where did your boyfriend go?" Corvus asked.

Eila explained what she'd tasked Lyrian with, then glanced at Grimrock. "I just wanted to add, I hope you don't feel like a burden. I'm happy you are with us." She smiled at Corvus. "I'm happy we are riding toward the end of the world together."

Corvus rolled his eyes. "Well-earned optimism from our fearless leader! I don't know about you, Grim, but I am fired up." His eyes widened. "Shit. Lyrian's heat. What am I going to do when his power…"

Eila lifted a bundle of cloth by her feet and tossed it to Corvus. The white cloak was thick and soft. "This warded cloak can stave off the elements for even the thinnest skin."

Corvus held the cloth before him, face sour. "You're kidding."

Eila shrugged. "Freeze, then. I thanked Agnes for providing it." She turned her attention to Blizzard and Glisten. "Okay, striders, *mush!*"

The cart jerked, rocking Corvus back. Eila had braced herself. Grimrock didn't shift.

Eila guided the striders into a wide turn. Soon, the abandoned buildings were behind them, and everything was white.

Here we are, Eila thought, *a banished faerie and her companions, riding toward the end of the world. I only hope that I keep my direction true and live to see my father again.*

Corvus was thinking the same thing as he stared at the back of Eila's head. However, all he could see was blue and red, and he heard Eila's screams as the powerful blast launched her into the abyss.

CHAPTER ELEVEN

Eila's heart hammered as they skimmed through the snow. She braced herself as the cart crested a hilltop, stomach lurching as it descended and gravity took effect.

The snowstriders trod confidently. Occasionally, they passed ghostly forests limned in violet as electrical pulses danced through the clouds.

Eila's adrenaline energized her as they put distance between them and the village. She had never been this far out in the realm, and it was amazing. At one point, Eila looked over her shoulder and laughed despite the seriousness of their situation. Grimrock might as well be a statue for all he moved as they rocked over bumps and dips.

Corvus almost blended with the snow, glowering out from under the hood of the thick white cloak. Eila had never seen him in anything but black, and she was enjoying the change.

"Problem?" Corvus spat.

"Sorry," Eila replied. "I thought we had a snowman riding with us." She winked, leaving Corvus to grumble.

The snowstriders made their need to rest known by stopping when a dense forest blocked their path. They lay down in the snow, but they still towered above Eila. She unhooked the reins to let them roam, and Blizzard licked her cheek before the pair trotted into the woods.

"Are you certain they will come back?" Corvus asked. "I'd hate to be stuck out here."

"Did you lose the ability to fly?" Eila returned with a sardonic grin.

"No," Corvus replied. "But that's not going to happen in this cloak. I'd freeze into a popsicle before I made it past that first ridge, and we can't leave Grim here."

"I am perfectly capable of handling my situation," Grimrock argued. "I survived in near-solitude for centuries. I would survive the walk to the Faerie Door."

Eila smirked as they hopped off the cart and investigated their surroundings. Trees barred their passage. In the gloom, they were dark silhouettes, their needles weighed down by snow. Little else indicated their location. There were no signs of life in the forest besides the snowstriders' grunts and snorts.

"I'm hungry," Corvus complained, appearing at Eila's side.

"That could be a problem," Eila returned. "Little grows this far out, even without the end of the world threatening."

Corvus frowned as his stomach rumbled. "Hey, big guy. I don't suppose you remembered to pack some snacks?"

Grimrock pulled a parcel out of his cloak. Where he had been storing it, Eila couldn't tell. It had just looked like a lumpy part of his body. With delicacy that belied his size, Grimrock pinched the opening wide, revealing a mass of multicolored snacks.

Corvus laughed disbelievingly. The stark contrast of the vivid colors of the candy bar wrappers was jarring amidst the snow. Corvus drew out a Crunchie bar, a Snickers bar, a bag of Maltesers, M&Ms, Skittles, and peanut brittle.

"I don't suppose you've got coffee in there?" Eila asked. She had little hope that Grimrock would have brought the beans she had learned to adore.

Grimrock dipped his hand in farther and drew out a metallic flask.

When he unscrewed the top, steam funneled into the air as the scent of arabica beans reached Eila's nostrils. "Oh, Grimrock, you glorious creature!"

"Be prepared," Grimrock stated, holding up three fingers on one hand.

Corvus chuckled. He was snarfing a Snickers bar. "Isn't that the Boy Scout thing? Be prepared?"

Grimrock poured coffee into the thermos' lid. "That's one appropriation, yes."

Corvus waited for Grimrock to expand, but the troll did not oblige.

They ate in relative quiet, with the wind whistling around them and intermittent pulses of light snaking above. Were it not for the trees, they could have been in an unknown realm, surrounded by white, with few landmarks and only the elements to contend with. As Eila struggled to bite off peanut brittle, she looked at her companions, wondering if she'd ever felt this satisfied and whole while she lived at the Winter Court.

"How are we going to get through the trees?" Corvus asked. "We can pretend to be Santa in his sleigh, but I doubt trees will be as susceptible to magic as chimneys are."

Eila looked at Grimrock questioningly. The troll waved a hand. The Crunchie bar was absurdly tiny in his grasp.

"I guess it's up to me to figure this one out," Eila muttered.

"Unless you can make the reindeer fly." Corvus smirked.

Eila didn't understand the joke. "They're snowstriders," she replied, flexing her wings. "I'll be back shortly."

She took off, her muscles working hard to penetrate the wind and snow. She peered through half-closed eyes as she followed the forest in one direction, staying to the front of the trees.

She wasn't sure how long she flew. Eventually, she made her

way back to Corvus and Grimrock, her wings struggling to carry her as she landed.

"Anything?" Corvus asked.

"Nothing," Eila replied, panting heavily. "Grim, another cup. Then I'll try the other way."

Grimrock obliged. Eila drank greedily, then darted into the air again. Either the wind had grown stronger, or her energy had faded. She fought to stay above the trees and flying in a steady line.

Be smart, Eila. The last thing you need is to be separated from the others. You need them to do this.

What if she couldn't find a way through? What if they had reached the end of their journey?

No, Eila steeled herself. *I haven't come this far to fail.*

Wind buffeted her, forcing her toward the trees. She could barely see the forest floor since mist covered the ground. She leaned in, fighting the wind as she attempted to fly back toward the tree line.

A whining howl erupted from the forest, and Eila scanned for its source. It reminded her of wolves or gloamhounds.

Not gloamhounds. Eila stated firmly. *None of those in Faerie.*

But there were wolves. Eila had heard tales of missing villagers' and farmers' bodies being found days after they were supposed to return home, snow covering their blood.

Another howl came from the opposite direction, sounding like it was coming from everywhere. Eila braced herself against another gust as it dragged her above the trees.

No! She fought back, but horizontal snow beat her in the face, and her muscles complained as she furiously flapped her wings.

A howl below her, this one sounding like a laugh.

Eila gritted her teeth, funneling her energy into flying back the way she had come. She wouldn't go out like this.

She gained a few meters before purple lightning stung her vision and thunder rolled. As if collaborating with the storm, the wolves howled, and the wind forced Eila back. She twisted to align herself, but the wind changed direction, forcing Eila down.

Eila shouted for help, hoping Grimrock and Corvus would hear her but knowing they wouldn't. She tried to align herself again, but the wind changed direction as if it had anticipated her. Eila careened toward the forest floor, twisting and whirling through the trees, narrowly missing trunks. Thin branches whipped her skin, and bark scratched Eila's cheek as she threw her body to the left.

A branch tore her jacket as she corkscrewed. Pain exploded in one temple as white light claimed Eila's vision.

She crashed into snow.

CHAPTER TWELVE

Her temple *hurt*. "Aw, shit!" Eila tested the wound before she opened her eyes. Something rough dug into her back. There was pressure around one of her thighs.

"Corvus?" Eila's voice was weak. "It's not funny anymore."

She blinked, but the world was still blurred. She groaned, and a light shone into her eyes, increasing the pain in her head. She let her neck loll against the rough surface.

"Where am I?" she asked, supporting her neck with one hand. Warmth spread in her direction. She narrowed her eyes to slits and focused on the person approaching her.

Eila swallowed dryly, aware it had stopped snowing and the only things that existed in this world were the person approaching, Eila, and the tree supporting her back.

As the person drew closer, the light dimmed. Waves of heat still rolled toward her. "Lyrian?" she asked, a dazed smile on her face. "You're always saving me."

"She told me where to find you," Lyrian replied, standing in all his glory before her. He kept sending pulses of his Summer power in her direction, thawing the snow and staving off the chill. "I couldn't have done it without her."

He looked ethereal, limned by his power. The smile on his face was slightly off-kilter, as if it had been drawn on with unsure hands.

Eila frowned. "Who? Lyrian, who are you talking about?"

Someone stepped out from behind Lyrian. Eila clapped a hand to her mouth to stifle her gasp. The woman was shorter than Lyrian, but no less proud in her stance. She wore ice-blue armor trimmed in pure white. Her long blonde hair was gathered over one shoulder and trailed across her chest. Her eyes—*Eila's* eyes—were a brilliant azure as that familiar face stared at her.

"Mum?" Eila murmured, barely believing the words on her lips.

Lysandra Snowshadow stepped alongside Lyrian with a maternal smile. The pair was mismatched.

Eila tried to stand, but pain flared in her leg, and she sank back down. Lysandra rushed forward, and got down on one knee, taking Eila's face in her hands. The scents of lavender and roseberries flooded Eila's senses, a combination she wasn't aware she had missed until it her memory sensors fired. Tears pricked her eyes.

"Mum?" she repeated.

"Eila," Lysandra replied, but her eyes flickered as though she were glitching on a digital screen. "I've missed you, baby."

"You died," Eila stated flatly, unsure of what to say. She was prepared for this moment. "You... They said you died."

Lysandra shook her head. "And leave you alone forever?" She shook her head. "Never in a million years."

Eila looked past Lysandra at Lyrian, who was smiling at them. "How is this possible?"

Lyrian's magic flared brightly, then sputtered as though drops of rain had fallen on a candle flame. "I found her in the woods, Eila." He pointed back the way he had come. "Out there. There's a hideout. She's been living there in secret for years, defending the borders of our realm."

"Is that true?" Eila asked her mother.

Lysandra nodded with the smile that had peered at Eila from the pictures in her room on to her face. "Sometimes we have to make great sacrifices to save the ones we love."

Pain flared in Eila's head. Lysandra stroked her wound with deft hands, attempting to soothe her. Eila felt like she had been punched in the gut. Out of the corner of her eye, she swore she saw Corvus in the shadows, watching with a warm smile. There one minute, gone the next.

"What happened to me?" Eila asked, trying to remember how she had gotten here. Why was she leaning against a tree, confronting her long lost mother and her Summer Court suitor.

"Nothing," Lysandra replied, stroking Eila's hair, eyes bright as another wave of pain racked Eila's body. She clutched her chest, struggling for breath as a cold wave ran through her despite Lyrian's attempts to heat her.

"Something's wrong." Concern laced Eila's brow. Lyrian frowned, his frame shaking and sputtering. The light pulsed so bright it blinded Eila before dimming. In that moment of light, Lyrian and her mother were just shadows and ice.

Someone shouted nearby.

Lysandra studied Eila's face hungrily. "Stay where you are, princess. Mummy's got you. Soon you'll be all better, I promise—"

Lyrian screamed into the sky, head dropped back. Not the scream of a faerie, but that of an animal in pain—a primal screech that broke the illusion. Two large shapes came through the trees around Eila.

The entity hovering before Eila did not resemble her mother. The creature was a shifting mass of frozen crystals and shadow, its body long and its mouth large. Its maw floated inches from Eila's chest, and a white aura was being sucked down its throat as her energy faded.

Behind this entity were half a dozen more. Some danced wistfully nearby, but the others watched the snowstriders that bolted toward them, bashing them aside as they screeched and howled.

Eila's vision blurred again. She wanted to swipe at the entity but couldn't. She couldn't lift her arms. She could only slump as what little energy remained nourished the creature.

"Eila!" a familiar voice called as a mass of darkness rushed toward the entity and collided with it. The creature skidded through the snow, its screeches joining the cacophony. The snowstriders whirled and kicked, targeting the frozen ghosts that were feverishly excited at the prospect of their next meal, though they twisted and writhed to escape the creatures' kicks and headbutts.

Eila's eyes rolled back as something crashed past her. She made out Grimrock's frame as he crouched and tore at whatever bound Eila's leg. The tree behind her vibrated as tendrilled roots retreated, then Grimrock scooped her up and carried her away.

"Let's go," he instructed Corvus. The ravenkin was uncomfortable as he straddled the animated snowstriders since he had no saddle. The frozen entities moved back, hovering just out of reach as Grimrock climbed atop the second snowstrider with Eila in his arms.

She breathed deeply, temple still throbbing, as the snowstriders galloped through the trees away from the haunting screeches of Eila's attackers. Eila wondered what in the Iron Wastes had happened, and where they were going now.

CHAPTER THIRTEEN

"Well, that's it. We're lost!" Corvus threw up his hands after stumbling off his snowstrider. The snow was deeper than anticipated, and he grunted when he landed. "Is she okay?" Concern laced Corvus' face as he glanced at Grimrock. The troll carefully climbed off his snowstrider which had not struggled under his bulk.

Grimrock put Eila down inside a small cave they had stumbled across. The entry was half the troll's height, but the ground was dry. "Eila?"

Eila stretched her neck, blinking away the fog that had come over her since the ghost creatures attacked. Though her energy was still low, it was returning.

"I've been better," Eila managed, rubbing her thigh and wincing. "Could really do with some Crystal Pool healing." She groaned, then massaged her temples. "What the hell were those things?"

"Frost wraiths," Grimrock answered. "Haunted entities that lurk in the wilderness. Sometimes described as ghosts or will o' the wisps. Neither is correct, yet those are closer to any description I've been able to give."

"'Frost wraiths?'" Corvus repeated.

Grimrock nodded.

Eila frowned, looking troubled.

"What is it?" Corvus asked.

"They…" Eila wondered how to describe the experience with Lyrian and her mother. It had seemed real, and she couldn't help but feel there was some truth to the visions she had seen. "They showed me things. I… Lyrian and…and my mother took care of me. It was so real. I could feel his heat, and I could *smell* her. It was like she was there."

Grimrock and Corvus exchanged concerned looks.

"It was just in your mind," Grimrock replied, bending to inspect her head wound. "Wraiths can manipulate reality. They tap into your secrets and exploit your greatest vulnerabilities. Then they drink your energy until you are drained, but it'll never fulfill them. No matter how much a wraith eats, they are doomed to starve. It is a fate worse than death."

Her greatest vulnerabilities. It made sense. Well, sort of. Eila's greatest pain was the memory of her mother. She wished she could have enjoyed more years with her. She could also accept Lyrian's presence. He had shown her love, and she felt bonded with him.

Why had Corvus been standing there, too?

"Well, it felt more than real," Eila replied, leaning closer to Corvus as he dabbed at her sticky temple with the corner of his cloak. He had dipped the cloth in snow and allowed it to melt to remove the clotted blood. Eila tried to shift, groaning when her leg throbbed. "Why does my leg hurt so much?"

Grimrock met her gaze. "The roots."

"Roots?" Eila asked, pressing for further explanation.

"What do you remember from before the wraiths?" he asked.

Eila remember her attempt to back away from the tree line. The wind and the snow flurries had conspired against her, dragging her off track, and she had crashed into the trees. This last memory was a blur, and she had no recollection of hurting her leg.

She described her journey to Grimrock as Corvus checked on the snowstriders, which patiently waiting.

"When you landed, you must have upset the trees," Grimrock explained. "There is a legend that the ancestors of modern-day flora sleep deep in the forests. When you crashed, you must have awoken the spirit within one of these trees, and its roots grabbed you. I had to tear off the roots to free your leg." He cautiously looked outside the cave, as if expecting the nearby trees to respond to his heinous deed. "How is it?"

"Sore," Eila answered, wincing as she flexed it. "Thank you so much for coming when you did."

"Don't thank us," Corvus turned to the snowstriders. "Thank *them*."

Blizzard and Glisten were nuzzling the snow away to reach the grass beneath.

Eila rose on unsteady feet and limped toward them, then stroked their faces in turn. "Thank you so much." Her eyes widened. "Where's Agnes' cart?"

"We took it to as clear a landmark as we could find. It's on a hillock near the tree line, tucked behind some sentinel stones," Grimrock explained.

Corvus shrugged. "I have no idea where that is in relation to where we are now." He looked around. "Anyone know?"

Eila studied the sky. Grimrock answered, "We head due west to the mountain. That direction."

Eila sighted down his finger. "We can return the cart and the snowstriders on the homeward journey. I'm good to go. I won't get further into Agnes' debt than I already am." She stroked Blizzard's neck. "Corvus and I will ride this guy. Grim, are you okay to ride Glisten?"

"Why does Grim get Glisten?" Corvus asked, drawing closer to the snowstriders.

Eila shrugged. "Glisten. Grimrock. They both begin with G. What do you want from me?" She hopped onto Blizzard with a flap of her wings. Grimrock mounted Glisten, who knelt to allow him to so do.

"I've just made the connection!" Corvus declared.

Blank looks.

Corvus sang, *"Dasher and Dance and Prancer and Vixen…"*

"Yeah?" Eila replied.

"Comet and Cupid and Donner and Blitzen…" Corvus finished, looking at them expectantly. When they didn't react as he had anticipated, Corvus pointed between the snowstriders. "Blizzard and Blitzen? Vixen and Glisten?"

Eila chuckled. Grimrock smiled.

"They must be where Santa's reindeer came from," Corvus decreed.

Eila rolled her eyes.

Grimrock shook his head. "What do you think the life expectancy of snowstriders is? It's far more likely that Agnes named her striders after the reindeer, not the other way around. Even then, I believe it was a coincidence—and a stretch at that."

Corvus' head sank. "Just saying…"

A howl erupted from the trees, and Eila shivered. The snowstriders walked deeper into the woods.

The forest was thick, the needles of the pines interlacing overhead, blocking the view of the gray and white sky. There were no landmarks to speak of and no way to identify how far they had come. All they had to mark their passage were the indents and trails the snowstriders had left behind.

"Grim?" Eila asked uncertainly.

The troll's face was set, brow furrowed in determination. "We are heading in the right direction."

Corvus whispered, "How does he know?"

"There are many things we don't know about Grim," she replied quietly. "I've heard about electromagnetic forces controlling compasses and calling to rocks. When we arrived in Faerie, Grim assured me he could feel them."

"Why wouldn't he tell us?" Corvus said.

Eila considered this. "We all have our secrets, Corv. You should understand that." The memory of Corvus releasing a powerful wave of shadow magic he had previously kept to himself appeared in her head.

Corvus appeared pacified by her response, and held onto Eila as they continued through the forest. The cries of unknown creatures provided the soundtrack for their journey. After several hours, they took a break. The snowstriders stayed close, though the howling and growls of wolves got louder. Eila was certain they were being followed, and given the stories she'd heard about icefang wolves, she didn't want to confront them.

They ate more snacks and drank more coffee. Grimrock set up a neat tripod and lit a fire that melted a pot of snow into drinking water. When the snowstriders and the paras were satisfied, they continued on. The ground began to rise, which made Eila hope they were heading in the right direction.

"Ahead," Grimrock announced, pointing.

Eila peered through the snow and fog. After a few more steps, the land rose to become a sheer cliff bedecked in ice. Icicles hung from the outcrops, making a large cave appear to be the jagged gaping maw of a giant beast.

"Mother, you've done it, Grim," Eila whispered. She thought about the illustrations and faded text in Grimrock's books. Then blue eyes and red fire filled her vision.

"This is the easy bit," Corvus stated. "Navigate the cave, slay the guardian, and grab the Heart. No problem." Although his words were confident, his face was not.

They hopped off the snowstriders after the pair drew to a stop, grunting and complaining. After the riders slid off, their giant steeds stood shoulder to shoulder, relaxing.

Eila looked them in the eyes, stroking their chins. "You served us well. I will not ask you to enter this domain. Please, go where you will. I hope you will return when we are ready to go back."

A long, low howl rent the air. Eila sighed as the snowstriders huffed. "Stay safe. Please."

Blizzard snorted, and Glisten nuzzled Eila's neck. Then they stamped away quickly.

Eila faced the opening. "The good news is, no one else found this cave yet."

Grimrock nodded. "How can you tell?" Corvus asked.

"If they had," Grimrock answered, "we would have heard the commotion from several miles away."

Eila frowned.

"What is it?" Corvus asked. The faerie looking small against the cave's looming entrance.

"The wolves," she replied. "They've gone silent."

Grimrock squared off with the mountain. "That's because little fish know they're little fish, and they are still in the face of the apex predators."

"Way to instill confidence in *our* mission," Eila managed, limping toward the opening. Although she was healing, her thigh throbbed dully with each step. "Come on. If your scroll is anything to go by, we've still got a way to go."

Corvus swallowed, steeling himself.

Grimrock paused, eyes narrowed. He wasn't sure if Eila and Corvus sensed it, the instincts of the fae having gotten watered down over the generations, but the power of the mountain vibrated in his blood and called to him. Every nerve in his frame sparked with life and told him to run.

The troll followed the other two into shadow and ice.

CHAPTER FOURTEEN

In the dark cave, the ground was uneven, each step a hazard. After Corvus stumbled and looked down to see a dark pit beside him, Eila lit the way by conjuring a glowing orb suspended above the palm of her hand.

The cavern was high and wide. The ceiling was decorated with thousands of stalactites, some as long as Eila's fingers, others double Grimrock's height. Were it not for the task they had yet to execute, it would have been beautiful since the gray and brown rock was interlaced with crystal-blue ice.

"You don't get this sort of thing in London," Corvus marveled, glancing at the ceiling.

Water dripped around them as they progressed. Clumps of mushrooms like wet leaves wrapped around rocks littered the ground, and as they passed a colossal underground lake, white lily pads floated on the surface. The stillness of the water made it mirror-like.

"How do they grow without sunlight?" Corvus queried.

Grimrock pointed at a large hole in the ceiling that let a small amount of light seep in. On a sunnier day, sunlight would gild the lake, providing the elements the plants needed to grow.

The path sloped down. After an hour of walking, Eila noticed something odd. "The ice…"

"What about it?" Corvus replied.

"It's gone." Eila looked around. While there were plenty of stalactites and stalagmites, there were none of the blue crystals that had bedecked the first half of their passage.

Corvus, who had removed his cloak without thought, looked at the white bundle in his arms. "It's warm in here."

Grimrock nodded. "Three guesses as to why." He glanced at Eila. "The guardian is close."

Eila frowned, seeing the gloom and fear in Grimrock's eyes. She hadn't seen those before, and they made her heart flutter. If Grimrock was afraid, she should be too.

Grimrock commanded, "This way."

The heat intensified with every step. The ground became more unpredictable as it sloped up, then down, and at some points, to the side. There were pits and holes around them, and they had to walk across a narrow stone bridge.

"Tread lightly," she warned, focusing on Grimrock. She wondered what would happen if he fell into the chasm below. Would he be able to reassemble himself, or would he die like anyone else would?

"Easy for you to say," Grimrock quipped.

Corvus took one step onto the bridge and shook his head. "Screw this." He transformed into a raven and flew across the gap, morphing back to human after he reached the other side. "There. Simple."

Eila smirked. "So much for sticking together."

"Hey, I'm all for that," Corvus replied. "What I'm not for is needlessly endangering myself when we know that the big guy will be fine. Ain't that right, Grim?"

As Grimrock threw the bundle at Corvus, something exploded nearby. The sound echoed around the cave, vibrating Eila's bones. The ground shook, and Eila and Grimrock wobbled.

Grimrock dropped to one knee to lower his center of gravity and placed a hand on the bridge to stabilize himself.

Another wave of sound rocked Eila again, and she flailed as she stumbled off-balance. Her stomach leapt into her mouth as she fell off the bridge and she twisted, adrenaline coursing through her as she fought to right herself. Her wings caught the air and slowed her descent.

She looked up, and her jaw dropped. Several stalactites and large rocks were falling toward her. She dashed beneath the bridge and hovered there, glad that Grimrock hadn't fallen. After the echo faded, and the last of the rocks vanished into the chasm, Eila let out a breath of relief and ascended, then darted to Corvus. He grinned and nodded at the troll.

Grimrock looked like a statue. One arm was above his head, and a stalactite jutted from it.

"Grim!" Eila ran toward him but stopped before she crossed the bridge.

Grimrock gritted his teeth as he lowered his arm. Keeping the stalactite in front of him, he walked across the bridge.

Eila waited on tenterhooks, fearing the tremors weakened the bridge's integrity. When Grimrock reached the other side, she ran to him. "Are you okay?"

Grimrock looked up for final threats and, seeing none, turned his attention to his arm. The stalactite had penetrated a few inches, and a gooey green substance trickled from the point of entry. Eila couldn't help but stare. The liquid was luminescent and somehow alien.

Grimrock grunted, wrapped his fingers around the stalactite, and gave a quick, sharp tug. The rock projectile pulled free, releasing more of the green goo. Eila assumed it was Grimrock's blood since it pooled in the space where the spike had been. The glow faded and the liquid hardened into smooth stone.

"Grimrock?" Eila started, not sure what to ask.

Grimrock glanced at her. "I am fine, Eila. It healed."

He rose to and walked past Eila as if nothing strange had happened.

"Wait!" Eila called. "Grimrock, what *was* that? How did you..."

Grimrock turned so suddenly that Eila ran into him. He placed a hand on her shoulder, looking affectionately into her eyes. "While curiosity might help us understand the fabric of this universe, not everything should be questioned. I am fine, and that is all you need to know. Questions can come later. Right now, we have an objective to complete."

There was no malice in his words. Grimrock smiled at Eila, and when she nodded, he motioned to Corvus. "Let's go, blackbird. We are close."

Corvus gritted his teeth. "*Ra*-ven."

"You know what concerns me?" Eila asked, wiping sweat off her brow an hour later. The cave walls shrank and expanded around them like lungs of a giant.

"What?" Corvus' eyes were narrowed. He had removed his leather jacket. "That it feels like we're inside an oven?" He blinked away the sweat that dripped into his eyes. "You now know what it's like to be those pastries and cakes you like so much! This'll be great inspiration for your cooking class."

"*Baking* class," Eila corrected. "But it's not that. Have you noticed that there's nothing other than fungus living in this cave? No bears, no wolves, or even insects on the walls. This place is barren."

"It is guarded," Grimrock stated.

Eila looked at him expectantly.

Grimrock took a few more steps before adding, "When a place is guarded, it defies the laws of nature. Given the increase in heat and the waves of warm air, creatures know better than to make this place their home."

"Yet here we are, walking into the lion's den," Corvus muttered, drawing Eila's eye. There was sweat on his forearms, and his T-shirt clung to his biceps. She couldn't help but note how toned Corvus was. The alluring bulge of his muscles had been hidden by his jacket.

Corvus met Eila's eye. She turned away.

"Not a lion," Grimrock corrected.

"I know, I know!" Corvus replied. "I wish it *was* a lion."

"Even if it was Leogion?" Eila replied, smirking.

Corvus cocked an eyebrow.

"Leogion is the Summer Court's sun god, Heliox's flaming familiar. It is said that Leogion can grow to the size of stars, emitting enough heat to melt the toughest iron found in the Wastes. A glimpse of Leogion's eyes would blind a king and melt him into a puddle."

Corvus smiled, impressed. "Wow, you faeries really know how to tell a story."

"You aren't familiar with fae culture?" Grimrock asked. He didn't have sweat glands.

"Not really," Corvus admitted. "My parents hated their exile and curse, so they were rather tight-lipped about their former home. They wanted us to adapt to the human world and forget our heritage. It makes things easier."

Eila shook her head. "That is a shame."

Corvus glanced at Eila. "Would you explain something?"

"That depends on the question," Eila replied with a grin.

"What are the Wastes you talk about? I assume they are the fae's hell, given the context in which you use it in, but I don't understand."

Eila's smile slipped. The Iron Wastes were a grim realm that held a painful meaning for the fae. "The Iron Wastes are worse than hell." Eila thought about Grimrock's description of the Christian hell as they discussed their battle with Maevis and Lilith. The flames and the demonic entity known as "Satan" were overlaid with images of the Iron Wastes. "In hell, you have fire and brimstone to burn you. The Wastes are cold, suffocating iron, stretching as far as you can see. No warmth, no magic, and no way out.

"It's a prison we can't survive. Iron strips us of our magic, our connection to nature, and our strength. It weakens us until we have no power or hope."

Her voice grew darker. "The Wastes aren't just a realm. They're a death sentence. Those who are sent there don't return. It's a fate worse than death."

Eila looked away. "So, when I speak of the Wastes, it's not just fear. It's the knowledge that no matter how strong or clever you are, the Wastes break everyone. Reduce you to component elements. Drink you dry."

They were quiet for a moment, footsteps echoing around the cave.

Corvus broke the silence. "The Iron Wastes are real?"

"As real as you and me," Eila replied.

The troll didn't look at Corvus.

"I knew the fae had an aversion to iron," Corvus murmured. "That's why I no longer use handcuffs in the bedroom."

Eila's ears pricked up, and she looked amused.

"But hell seems theoretical," Corvus continued. "There is no way to prove its existence. Damn. That's a lot to take in."

"It is a nightmare," Eila stated, then started. There was a dull orange glow ahead.

Grimrock muttered, "We are about to walk into one."

Corvus swallowed dryly.

Eila steeled herself.

"The guardian?" Corvus asked.

Grimrock took a deep breath. "I can only guess."

Eila's clothes felt too tight when a wave of heat washed over them. "I'd rather go out in a blaze of glory than stand with my knees knocking, delaying the inevitable." She strode ahead of Grimrock and Corvus. "We've got a job to do. Let's get it done."

A low rumble made the floor shake. Eila wondered if the cave had chuckled.

CHAPTER FIFTEEN

The glow got brighter as the cave descended. The heat and the light intensified until Eila wished for a moment outside in the blizzard. Her tongue stuck to the roof of her mouth, and her steps were labored. She and Corvus shielded their eyes with their forearms until they reached a new cavern.

Fire and ice filled the opening, as though Leogion was barring entry. The cave rippled in the heat. Eila tried to speak, but no words would come.

"What now?" Corvus asked.

"Now we cross the barrier." Grimrock stared determinedly ahead. His stony gray exterior glowed as though the rock that made up his skin was turning into lava.

"Eila, this is your time," Grimrock declared.

Eila gave a determined nod, then stood before the veil. She spread her arms and formed a bubble of light and snow and ice large enough to protect Corvus and Grimrock as well. Corvus gasped as he enjoyed the sweet relief of the cold. Grimrock's skin returned to its usual gray.

"Why didn't you do this earlier?" Corvus asked. "My gods, this is wonderful."

Eila didn't reply, focusing on the way in. Waves of heat crashed into her, trying to disrupt the protective ward she had cast.

"To save energy," Grimrock explained.

Corvus slipped on his jacket and the cloak when the cold soaked into his bones. He and the troll stayed close to Eila as the doorway loomed closer.

Eila took one step, then another, and another, her energy draining. When her globe met the barrier, light erupted around them and magic filled the air as though they were standing beneath a waterfall holding an umbrella. Eila thought about walking beneath Fenris' waterfall, wishing she could take a swift dip in the Crystal Pool to energize herself for what lay ahead.

She pressed on, the weight of Grimrock's and Corvus' welfare heavy on her shoulders. If she failed, Corvus might burn to ash, and Grimrock would melt into a pool of lava. She held her arms straight out and gritted her teeth until a scream threatened to erupt from her throat. With a loud *pop*, the light faded, and the world grew quiet.

Eila cautiously stepped forward, reluctant to lower the shield. They were looking into a large, enclosed cavern, the walls thick with ice covered with dancing blue and white flames. Stairs descended to the floor of the chamber, and there was a large, uneven platform in the center.

In the middle of the platform was a dais with something floating above it. The object hovered and winked, unidentifiable from where they stood.

"The Heart?" Eila breathed.

"Yes," Grimrock confirmed, his eyes betraying his disbelief. Perhaps he had doubted its existence despite the tales and legends in his books.

"Where's the guardian?" Corvus asked.

There was nowhere to hide.

"Could it have escaped through the veil?" Eila asked,

wondering if luck was with them and the monstrous guardian she had seen in Grimrock's books was gone. According to the stories, the guardian and the Heart had been placed here thousands of years ago. Was the Heart now unguarded, the spell that had bound the monster broken?

"I wouldn't trust to hope," Grimrock stated, nostrils flaring. "There's magic here. I can smell it in the air."

"Let's make this quick!" Corvus took his crow form.

Eila tracked the raven as he sped toward the dais. He got to the platform in seconds and transformed a few feet from the artifact. Eila could only imagine the glint in his eye when he saw the treasure. Being a raven, he immediately reached for the shiny object.

He cried out and retracted his hands when white fire erupted. He flew back several feet and landed painfully on his rump. He tried to beat out the flames on his sleeves on the icy floor, but the fire would not be quelled. He then called to Eila, who was already rushing to his aid.

Corvus' face was a mask of pain. Despite the ice, the flames continued to rage. The ice didn't melt, remaining hard and indifferent.

"Eila!" Corvus called as the stink of burned flesh reached Eila's nose. She knelt beside Corvus and put her hands around his wrists, and pain flared in her palms. The fire was greedy. Eila's eyes rolled back, but she did not let go. She used her power to prevent the flames' spread. Corvus writhed in her grip as she focused, ignoring the pain as she muttered beneath her breath.

The pain diminished as the flames under Eila's fingers shrank. She held on until she was certain Corvus' pain was gone. The ravenkin relaxed in her grasp.

Eila sat back, the cold uncomfortable even for her. Corvus slumped, hands held out before him, revealing red welts around his wrists. His jacket's sleeves were gone to the elbow.

"Are you okay?" Eila asked, though there was no good answer to that question.

"*Fuck*," Corvus shouted. The word bounced around the room. "*Fuck! Fuck! Fuck!*"

Corvus awkwardly levered himself into a sitting position, then stared at his wrists. He couldn't rest them on his legs, and as they hovered in front of him, he hissed. "You'd think that after the ice and snow, I'd be thankful for a little heat." He looked around as if expecting to find a first aid kit. "What the hell was that?"

Eila turned her attention to the Heart. "Defense ward," she guessed. There was a dream-like quality to her voice. The Heart of Frostfire lazily bobbed up and down as it hovered. A glittering ice-blue aura surrounding the artifact, which was crafted of gold and rubies and diamonds and sapphires. Its power danced across the surface in a flash of blue fire as if warning Eila against what she had to do.

"I didn't bring any tongs. They might have made this easier." Corvus grunted and rose, trying not to use his hands. "Shit, that's painful. You think this is what the iron in the Wastes feels like?"

Eila couldn't take her eyes off the jewel. "Possibly."

Grimrock reached the platform. "Are you okay?"

"I've been better," Corvus admitted. He winced as pain flashed across his wrists. "I'm going to need a long dip in the Crystal Pool when this is over. I don't suppose anyone brought aloe vera?"

Grimrock shook his head.

"Shit," Corvus stated flatly. "Eila, are *you* okay?"

Eila had risen and was standing before the Heart. Its glow lit her face, and although it shouldn't be possible, something whispered to her in a language she didn't comprehend. It prickled her skin and set her curiosity aflame.

"Careful," Corvus stated. "I know you're all icy and whatnot, but ice melts, sister."

Eila wasn't listening. Although she had never before laid eyes on the Heart of Frostfire, the item seemed familiar. She felt like she knew the artifact and had seen it before. Had owned it in a previous life.

Eila reached for it, hands shaking.

A booming voice shattered the quiet.

"A heart of ice, and a heart of flame.

A weapon to wield in the master's grand game!"

The cave shook, and Eila noticed there were no icicles or stalactites hanging from the ceiling and no stalagmites growing out of the ground. Jagged diamonds decorated the roof, each as wide as Eila's wingspan.

They looked like scales.

Grimrock stared up. Corvus stumbled, flailing his arms to regain his balance.

"Two forces for evil, two weapons for kind.

A power that will corrupt the mind!"

Eila looked around, but could not explain the voice. It was as though the cave was speaking…until she saw the huge eyes open.

Each slitted pupil was the height of Grimrock. The eyes blinked, and the cave shifted as the beast unfurled. They were not in a cavern. They stood within the coils of a beast, trapped after they passed through the veil.

The creature turned its head to them, and a dark cavern of a mouth appeared as the it smirked. Its fangs would tear muscle and break bone. Eila's breath caught as she stared at Frostfang.

The dragon was ice-blue in some places and snow white in others. The flames that formed the barrier danced across the dragon's body, and the spiky scales that trailed down its spine were the size of sails.

The dragon sneered at Eila, its warm breath rank. "Well met, fellow traveler," Frostfang crooned, its voice deep and gravelly. "It has been nigh on a millennium since my last visitor."

"Fr-fr-frostfang?" Eila asked, alarmed.

"Indeed," the dragon replied.

Corvus stared at it, wide-eyed. Grimrock stopped beside her, bringing Eila back to her senses. She calmed down. "We have come for the Heart," Eila began, the confidence back in her voice.

"Why would you steal my treasure?" Frostfang returned, bristling. "You may have found my domain, but you must know I won't allow you to take it."

"The world is under threat," Eila explained. "The sky is filled with a strange power, and the realms are dying. Evil conspirators are trying to gather the magical items, and should they get their hands on the Heart, I fear the world as we know it will end."

The dragon's eyebrows twitched. "The Heart shall not be removed, not by you and not by another. For centuries, I have guarded the jewel, and I shall guard it for millenia more. You have one chance to escape with your lives before I demonstrate my *power!*"

Frostfang's voice rose as something moved behind Eila. She turned to find Corvus' eyes locked on the Heart. He reached for it, burned arms stretched before him. Eila shouted, "*No!*" but it was no use. Corvus' curse betrayed him, and he reached for the shiny object.

Something white whipped up and barred his way and his view. The tip of Frostfang's tail was thick and scaled. Eila knew it would pierce flesh like a heated knife went through butter.

Frostfang's slitted pupils flickered from Corvus to Eila. "One chance, faerie. I advise you to take it."

Eila sighed, images flashing in her mind as she gazed at Corvus and Grimrock. She saw the Winter Court, its brilliant blue walls and icy chambers filled with the sharp-featured faces of her kin. She saw herds of mooncalves in the fields below her balcony. She saw her mother's face, and lavender and roseberries tickled her nostrils. She saw her father reading in his study. Aria and Lyrian filled her vision, followed by the fields at the Summer Court. Those morphed into the faerie doors that had taken Eila to her new home.

Then she saw London, skyscrapers stretching above her. She saw Grimrock typing on his behemoth machine and Ozzie crawling from his jar. Corvus chased his brothers around their apartment as Hayley brandished an admonishing finger. She tasted cake and saw Leonie smirking beside her. Agnes slipped into her mind at the last minute.

Then she saw Silas' face as she stood in the heart of the Winter Palace, scared and confused but accepting her fate. The smirk on Silas' lips filled her with anger as the image shifted to a wrathful boil of purple power that zagged through stormy clouds.

She couldn't turn around after all she had been through. Eila had this one chance to prevent what would come to pass if she failed, and if she had to fight this dragon to succeed, that was what she would do.

"I'm sorry," Eila whispered to the dragon. Its ears perked to catch the sound. "There is only one path."

Eila's palms flashed, and ice daggers whistled toward Frostfang's eyes. Her wings vibrated as she leapt over the dragon's tail and seized the Heart of Frostfire.

All hell broke loose.

CHAPTER SIXTEEN

Frostfang's roar vibrated their bones. Chunks of ice broke off the walls of the cavern and crashed to the floor.

Grimrock and Corvus planted their feet when the ground rumbled and threw them off-balance. Grimrock crouched, using one hand to steady himself. Corvus shifted to raven form, and shadows cloaked him. He twisted and danced to escape the falling rock and debris.

That all happened behind Eila as she clutched the Heart of Frostfire to her chest. The light artifact thrummed in her hands. She had expected flames to attack her as they had Corvus, but a white glow shone from within and the Heart beat in her hands, causing her heart to race.

Eila landed next to the dais and spun to face the dragon. Fire boiled out of Frostfang's mouth, half blue, half orange, forming a yin-yang of ice and flame.

Eila's skin prickled as the light from the Heart and its desperate thumps propelled her forward. Her hands glowed, and Eila gasped when a blue shield appeared in her left hand and a sleek silver-white longsword appeared in her right.

Eila stepped in front of Grimrock, crying out for Corvus to

stand behind them, and they all ducked behind the shield as a torrent of fire that was both searing hot and freezing cold surrounded them. The shield miraculously held the fire at bay, though Eila was pushed back by its force.

The flames blinded them, and Eila wondered how long she could hold on. When she looked down at her chest, she saw that the Heart was resting against her as though it had melded into her clothes.

Grimrock growled. Corvus squawked. Frostfang continued to belch the conflagration like it would never stop.

Then it did. Frostfang's onslaught died. Through her new shield, Eila saw a distorted dragon. Frostfang was now only three times Grimrock's height. Although it was terrifying, its scales glittered like jewels, and its wings were snow white.

"The first test was passed," Frostfang announced. "Few can withstand the Heart's power. Your friend failed to harness its wrath."

"Test?" Eila asked, her gaze flicking to the flaming portal that would let them go back the way they had come. "This was planned?"

"Planned?" Frostfang chuckled. "Oh, no, Eila Snowshadow. In an infinite universe, there can be no plans, only possibilities, and we must be prepared for every eventuality. What you hold grants great power, and none who are unworthy may wield it."

Eila glanced at the glowing Heart, whose golden aura streamed into her. Her fears were allayed by its beating. She brought the shield closer to her body and held the icy sword out. She would conquer their foe and leave the chamber.

"What is the second test?" Eila asked, knowing the answer before the words left her mouth.

The dragon smirked, and smoke plumed out of its nostrils. "Defeat me." No sooner had the dragon finished its sentence than it sped toward Eila.

Eila met it halfway and slammed the shield into its snout, preventing it from crashing into Grimrock and Corvus.

The dragon's bulk knocked Eila askew, and she slid across the icy platform on her belly. She flipped around, and launched into the air, then put some distance between her and the dragon.

Frostfang belched blue and orange flame as it roared, and the fire struck the icy walls, creating more blue crystals.

Eila closed her eyes, embracing the power of the Heart as she pointed her sword at the dragon. The weapon throbbed, and a bolt of ice and snow sped at Frostfang's chest. Its scales shielded its chest, and the beam dissipated.

Frostfang laughed. Another column of flame flew at where Eila was hovering. She twisted out of its path, her hair rippling from its power as she attempted to outmaneuver the beast. She was like a fly against a mooncalf, the beast weighed down by its bulk while Eila evaded it using her litheness and agility.

A rush of adrenaline hit her, and she wondered when she had last stretched her wings and reveled in the wind whipping past her. Had it truly been when she was flying across Faerie to her exile? Now she felt free and powerful, unbound by the whims and demands of anyone else.

Frostfang's flames threw her into the wall and exploded around her. Its rough surface was hard under her cheek as the fire pinned her in place. The dragon's growl got louder as it approached, but the Heart thrummed against her chest, protecting her. However, she couldn't escape, and all the magic in the world would be useless if Frostfang ate her.

Eila pressed her hands to the ice, her aching muscles useless under the assault. She heard indistinct shouts, and as she opened her eyes, something black swept by.

Corvus soared toward the dragon, the raven a fly compared to an elephant. Frostfang paid him no heed until Corvus shifted into human form in midair to cast a spell. He hovered as a stream of shadow laced with something red and sparkling flew at Frostfang's eyes. As Corvus descended, he shifted back to raven form, then darted around the dragon to avoid its wrath.

Frostfang roared again, suspending his attack on Eila.

The ice scratched her cheek as she kicked off the wall and sprang back into the air. She sped toward the creature, teeth gritted and eyes narrowed. As she approached, Frostfang snapped his mighty jaws shut, but Eila pivoted, the gust propelling her away. She gained height, then pointed the sword at Frostfang's head, dumping ice and snow on top of it.

Frostfang flinched and spun to face her. Eila descended toward the ground, smirking.

"You have a lot of fight, faerie," Frostfang declared. "It's a shame I have to exterminate you. Few soldiers have your constitution, but they make a delicious meal. Meager, but welcome."

Eila sank lower. Frostfang paced her, and they touched down. "Make it easy on yourself, Eila," the dragon suggested. "Accept your fate."

Eila clenched her teeth. "I can't do that."

"Very well." Frostfang sounded bored. "Then I shall take you down."

Corvus flew above its head, not on the dragon's radar. Eila winked, then hurled her shield at the dragon.

Caught off-guard, it flinched as the shield crashed into its snout. The flying metal caused no damage, but the impact distracted the dragon.

Eila surged up, and it growled, eyes locked on the faerie. It flapped its great wings and launched into the air…

Then jerked to a halt. It struggled to remain aloft as it examined what anchored it to the ground. Grimrock held Frostfang's tail, preventing it from ascending.

Frostfang roared in frustration, creating flames in its throat as Corvus descended toward it, shifting to cast another spell. Darkness blinded the dragon.

Frostfang sent fire in all directions, and when he roared,

debris fell off the walls and ceiling. Grimrock twisted and slammed Frostfang's body into the platform in a move like that of a wrestler Corvus had shown Eila on his phone.

"*Now!*" Eila shouted.

Corvus landed on Frostfang's back and, shifting to shadow, stretched his arms to either side. Darkness poured out of his hands and wrapped around the dragon's wings' tips, then solidified into black chain links that thrummed with red electricity. Corvus' eyes rolled back to show their whites as he maintained the chains.

Frostfang spewed another jet of fire as he fought to face Corvus.

Corvus pulled his arms together, dragging the wings by the chains until they were tethered to the dragon's body. Corvus' knees buckled when the surge of power drained his body, but he threw his arms out, binding the chains to the platform to hold Frostfang in place.

Grimrock released the dragon's tail. It thrashed and caught Grimrock with a claw, sending him flying over the edge of the platform and out of sight.

"*Grim!*" Eila shrieked. She wanted to run to him, but she had to neutralize the threat. She landed in front of Frostfang, dodging his intermittent bursts of flame. She held out her arm, and the shield flew back to her. Standing erect, she snapped, "Enough!"

The dragon's eyes blazed with fury as it struggled against its bonds. The dragon shifted to the side and Corvus fell off, as limp as a rag doll.

Frostfang's furious eyes locked with Eila's. "You know not what it is you do," it warned.

"I have to save my world," Eila returned. "And this is the only way."

"If you take that artifact out of here, you will deliver it into the hands of the enemy." The dragon snorted. "Then you will not be able to stop what is coming."

"I will know I tried," Eila shot back. She looked at the restrained dragon with pity. "We are leaving now. You cannot stop us."

To her surprise, the dragon grinned. "I was told that one day, a faerie would arrive who was worthy of my best. I had begun to believe that day would never come. The Heart of Frostfire has corrupted many minds, yet here you stand. Though I would still like to kill you, I admire you, Snowshadow. You have a stout heart, and that is rare in these evil times."

Eila lowered the shield. "Thank you. I only wish to save my people."

"Then go," Frostfang commanded, pointing its snout at the writhing portal. "You might have to leave your friends. They are in no condition to travel, and I am hungry."

Eila's compassion faded when she saw that Corvus was in a pile beside the dragon, face-down on the ice. His chest heaved, and his arms bore the black marks of his power.

Where was Grimrock? Eila looked over the edge of the platform. He should have returned by now. How far was the fall, and how much damage could he take?

"If you want to save the world, you will walk alone," Frostfang repeated, reveling in Eila's concern. "Don't you worry about your friends. I'll look after them. I so enjoy keeping pets." His slitted pupils dilated and contracted hungrily.

Eila growled and ran to Corvus. Frostfang snapped his jaws at her to block her way, but she slashed with the sword. The dragon barely managed to twist out of the way in time.

"It's you alone or no one," Frostfang repeated. "Make your decision. Sacrifices are always required."

Eila's stomach knotted. She had come this far with Corvus and Grimrock and had envisioned them standing by her side when they were hailed as heroes. Was this the only way? The portal glowed behind her, illuminating the cavern. Could saving the world be as simple as flying out the door?

She couldn't do that. After everything that they had been through and the effort and sacrifices Corvus and Grimrock had made to accompany her, she wouldn't let them fall at the last hurdle. If they won, they would do it together.

Mother be damned.

"No," Eila stated, and the Heart glowed. Light erupted around Eila as she stared into Frostfang's eyes, twisted delight settling on its features.

"Third test passed," Frostfang declared. Its body rippled with excitement. "Now comes the final test, and this one you will *not* pass."

Corvus' chains snapped and Frostfang stood, growing as it roared. The darkness and shadow that had bound him flowed back into Corvus, who remained on the ground as the dragon's throat filled with fire.

Eila held the shield before her, blinded as a fire that matched Legion's rained down upon her. Power she had never before felt erupted and she was cocooned, unable to hear the scream that burst from her throat.

Impossibly, she did not feel the fire.

CHAPTER SEVENTEEN

I should be dying, Eila thought. *I should be crumbling into ash and melting into the ground.*

She wasn't, so she roared in an attempt to match Frostfang's cries. Her feet were seemingly glued to the ground as she held the shield before her, the sword by her side.

She stepped forward.

The dragon's power struggled to push her back.

Eila stepped forward again, focused on reaching the dragon. The world was white and it stung her eyes, but she took step after step after step until she reached Frostfang's stomach.

She brought the sword high, ignoring the glimmering blue that encased her arm as she swung, ice and steel meeting dragon flesh. A scale ripped off Frostfang's stomach, and it cried out, flapping its wings to attempt to buffet her back. Eila stabbed, and the blade pinned Frostfang's foot to the ice. He struggled to maneuver out of her reach but failed.

Not today, Eila thought stubbornly. A dagger appeared in her hand, and she threw the shield aside. A second dagger appeared in her now-free hand, both made of ice or crystal. Eila couldn't tell which.

Frostfang's face wore a mask of pain, its fiery assault broken. Eila followed her instincts and thrust a dagger into its stomach. As the dragon howled, she inserted in the second dagger higher than the first to ascend her his frame.

"*Nooooo!*" Frostfang roared, confused and panicked, then breathed fire at her. The Heart thrummed, radiating that brilliant white glow that protected her. Eila scaled its chest as Frostfang struggled to free its foot and reached its shoulders a moment later.

Eila balanced herself, then thrust both daggers into its neck. Though they couldn't sink deep into its flesh, fear flared in Frostfang's eyes as Eila climbed up to reach its head.

Frostfang belched fire and screamed bloody murder. As it whipped its head around, Eila grabbed its horns, holding herself steady as she looked around the cave. Corvus was a speck on the ground, but still no Grimrock.

Frostfang reared, neck straining as it aimed its fire at the ceiling. "This will not come to pass!"

Eila turned her attention back to the beast. "I'm afraid you have no choice." She crouched, gripping its horns, then closed her eyes, listening to the Heart's whispers as she muttered. Power poured from her, then flowed across Frostfang's horns and down his body.

The dragon froze in terror. "*No! No!*"

He fell forward, landing on all fours. That jarred Eila but did not break her focus. A moment later, she sat on white light in the shape of the dragon.

Eila's eyes snapped open, glowing white with no pupils. She screamed at the ceiling, the last of the spell taking effect as she released her grip on Frostfang's horns. She slid off its head and landed clumsily on all fours, panting.

Frostfang lay still. Eila got her breath as silence filled the cave. Then she looked at the ice statue lying beside her.

"Holy..." she muttered. The dragon was enshrouded in ice,

frozen to the platform. She could make out its features beneath a thick outer layer that, in this frigid cave, would take years to melt—if it ever did.

Eila placed a hand on the ice and started when something swam beneath it. The dragon's eyes had moved.

You did well, Eila Snowshadow, it said in her head. *I do not condone your methods, but you proved your strength and your heart. Go now to where you are needed most. The only location where the world can be saved.*

Eila frowned. "What do you mean? I have the Heart."

Yes, but you cannot stop the storm. Treasures will be united, no matter what you do. I saw what your friend saw, and unless you break the enemy, the end will find come.

Eila ran her fingers through her hair. "Just stop with the riddles. What must I do?"

Mount the Crest of the Gods and face your true enemy, Frostfang instructed. *Where the peak is highest, an end will come. Whether it is good or ill is for you to decide.*

Eila shook her head, irritated. She was about to ask more questions when Corvus groaned. Eila went over to him. "Corvus, it's okay. I'm here," She rolled him onto his back. His eyes were bloodshot, and his arms bore black lines.

He shivered, the cold setting in now the battle was won. "Did we w-win?"

"Yes," Eila replied, but there was no conviction in her words after Frostfang's revelation. "Let's get you home and warm."

Eila searched for Corvus' cloak and let out a startled chuckle when Grimrock walked toward them with the cloak in his arms. Well, in one arm. The other was a lump of rock missing from his bicep. The glowing green goo was attempting to heal him. "Looking for this?"

Eila ran over and hugged the troll. She didn't note the admiring look he gave her when she sped back to Corvus to lay the cloak over him. "We need to get out of here. Grim, can you carry him?"

The ice-encased dragon chuckled. *Good luck* it said inside Eila's head as the cave trembled. The vibrations built up, and debris and rocks rained down from the ceiling. She yelled for Grimrock to hurry, and the troll scooped up their injured companion.

"*Run!*" Eila shouted, desperate to fly through the portal but determined not to leave her friends behind. She cast a ward of protection as she followed Grimrock, whose focus was on the fiery door.

Boulders and blocks of ice attempted to block their path, but they navigated their way around, the progress painfully slow. "*Come on! Almost there!*" Eila cried as the portal's flames filled their vision. As they stepped toward the threshold, a final message came into Eila's head.

Well-fought, Eila Snowshadow. Until next we meet...

Grimrock grunted beside her as they exited Frostfang's lair.

CHAPTER EIGHTEEN

Eila had hoped leaving the cave might be easy, but that was not the case. The outer cave shook, more rocks and rubble raining down on them as she encouraged Grimrock forward. She kept maintaining the protective ward, but her energy faded fast.

They wove through the tunnels and caverns and raced over the questionable bridge as rock turned to ice on the walls. Eila broke out in sweat. She wished Grimrock could run faster. Each second she held the ward pained her, and it now twitched in and out of existence.

Frostfang's wrath followed them. Eila stumbled and landed on one knee. Grimrock pulled her to her feet, Corvus' body dangling limply over one arm. "Almost there," the troll encouraged, though Eila wasn't sure if that was true. She groaned, then continued, slower than before, using the last dregs of her power.

The mouth of the tunnel beckoned ahead, giving her the kick she needed. They staggered outside, then fell into the soft powder. Rocks filled the cave's entrance, leaving barely enough space for anyone to pass through, but Eila didn't care. She was free. She had saved Grimrock and Corvus, and she had the item they'd come to acquire.

She lay on her back in the snow, staring at the thick cotton blanket that covered the sky. The Heart beat rapidly to begin with, slowing as its power withdrew into the item.

Grimrock peered at her, then set Corvus down beside her.

"Corvus? Are you okay?" Eila asked.

To her delight, Corvus blinked, groaning as he fought to keep his eyes open. "I've been better."

Eila examined her friend. The white cloak covered most of his body, but his arms were exposed, the fur singed at the edges. The ravenkin's veins were dark, lines drawn on his skin in corruption as he had cast his magic to save them. His wrists and arms and hands were burned, and he placed them in the snow and breathed a sigh of relief.

"Thank you," was all Eila could think of to say.

"You're wel—" Corvus began. He was forced to stop when Eila placed her lips on his and stole his breath.

Almost immediately, Eila drew back, cheeks flushing. She wasn't sure what had come over her, but seeing him in pain in the snow after risking his life to save them, she couldn't fight the flood of emotion that rose. Corvus had sacrificed himself for *her* mission.

Corvus smirked awkwardly, at a loss for words for the first time. As he tried to push up to a sitting position, shivering from the cold, he glanced at Grimrock. The troll had turned away.

"How you doing, big guy?" Corvus asked. "You took quite the fall back there."

Eila cleared her throat, then scratched the back of her neck.

Grimrock ignored the question. "We must move. Our enemies will be upon us soon. Time is of the essence."

"Wh-where are we going?" Corvus stuttered.

There was a knowing look in Grimrock's eyes. Frostfang had spoken to Eila in her head, but she was certain the troll knew things he hadn't shared.

"We need to go to the Crest of the Gods," Eila stated flatly.

Corvus cocked an eyebrow. "Another mountain? Why? We have the Heart. We did what we needed to do."

Grimrock held Eila's gaze. She straightened, pushing past her pain. "First, we have to find Lyrian. I promised I'd meet him."

Grimrock bristled. "Given the urgency of our quest, don't you think we should prioritize the task at hand?"

"We'll need to go back," Eila stated. "Corvus won't survive in this cold."

"The palace is farther than the Crest."

Corvus looked afraid. "We can't go up the mountain. Eila, you can't. It's not safe."

"I will do what needs to be done," Eila admonished, ignoring his fear. "And enough of this delaying. We need to get Corvus somewhere safe. That cloak will keep him warm, but with his arms exposed, he's at risk of frostbite."

Eila turned to the troll. "And who said we were going to the palace? The palace *is* too far, but the place I'm thinking of isn't."

Grimrock looked at her curiously.

Corvus shivered. "Wherever we're g-going, can we get a m-move on? I'm not ready to freeze into a popsicle."

Eila held out a hand. Grimrock silently removed his cloak and handed it to Eila. There were heavy bundles in hidden pockets, but Eila ignored them, focusing on wrapping Corvus up and ensuring his arms were covered. When Corvus was swaddled, breath misting in front of his face, she looked around. "Where are the snowstriders?"

Grimrock squared up to the trees, placed two fingers between his lips, and blew sharply. Eila didn't hear a whistle, but dark birds shot into the sky.

Blizzard and Glisten ran to them as long howls rang from the forest. "Shit," Eila muttered. "Grimrock, help me with him."

Grimrock scooped Corvus into his arms as if he weighed nothing and hopped onto the waiting Blizzard. Eila hopped onto

Glisten, flapping her wings as a jolt of purple energy sailed across the sky, and a clear, long howl sounded nearby.

Eila nudged Glisten in the flank as the first of the wolves arrived. They were almost invisible against the snow, though their eyes were like black charcoal, and their maws dribbled saliva. She had never seen the creatures in person, but the story books she had been raised on had done a great job of conveying their terror.

First there was one, then two. A dozen wolves warily stalked closer as the snowstriders stamped their feet.

"I thought you said they wouldn't come close to the mountain?" Eila asked Grimrock.

Grimrock stared at the wolves. "Nature is unpredictable."

Eila leaned forward and ran a hand along Glisten's neck. "Let's go."

The snowstrider leapt forward, but Blizzard sped past her and took the lead. Roars, barks, grunts, and hoofbeats rang out as they entered the forest. Eila held on tight.

Eila crouched over Glisten's neck as they wove between towering snow-covered trees. Branches whipped her face. Glisten leapt over roots and snowdrifts, but the wolves cut through the forest like shadows.

The trees offered some cover, but the narrow paths made their escape treacherous. When Glisten's hooves struck the unforgiving ground, Eila felt every impact.

"The forest should slow them!" Grimrock called back uncertainly.

"They're too close!" Eila shouted, turning to glance behind her. The sleek wolves darted through the trees with preternatural speed. Their dark eyes glinted as they expertly avoided the underbrush.

Eila's pulse quickened. She couldn't afford to panic, but she tightened her grip on the reins, urging her mount to go faster.

The cold air stung her cheeks, but she couldn't focus on anything other than the growls behind her.

"We have to slow them down!" Eila muttered a spell under her breath, weaving ice into the air around her, then sending it forward. Frost crept over the trees, creating a lattice of ice that spread across the ground.

Grimrock fixed his gaze ahead, determined to keep them on track. Corvus twisted back to Eila, scanning the pack that barreled toward them. "I'll try to block their path!"

"Corvus, no!" He had already used too much power.

Corvus raised a hand, and the shadows seemed to bend toward him. With a quick motion, he sent dark tendrils snaking through the trees, creating barriers and traps between the trunks. The wolves snapped and howled as they collided with the darkness, some getting tangled in the shadow webs.

His magic slow the closest wolves. "It won't hold them for long," Corvus muttered, his breathing ragged from the effort.

Eila glanced back as the wolves began their pursuit anew. She had no idea where they were heading, with only trees, snow, and shadows to go by.

When they encountered a stream that expanded to a river, Grimrock called over his shoulder. "This might be a ravine leading down the mountain and out of the forest!"

Eila pressed closer to Glisten, urging her forward. The snowstrider's muscles worked hard beneath her, her breath coming out in misty puffs.

They followed the river, the howls and yips behind them growing louder and sharper. Eila's pulse raced. The wolves weren't giving up, but the trees thinned ahead.

"Almost there," Eila whispered to Glisten. Blizzard appeared to respond to her declaration as well, and she remembered Agatha's words about snowstriders responding to fae intentions. She let herself believe they would make it out without further wounds, but that hope was shattered the moment a massive shadow darted out of the trees to her left.

Eila's heart lurched as a wolf that was twice the size of the rest of his pack charged them. His fur was a swirling mix of white and dark gray that seamlessly blended with the snow and forest, eyes a blazing yellow compared to his brethren. Frost coated his snout as a long, rumbling growl warned them of his intentions.

"You see him, Eila?" Corvus shouted.

Before Eila could answer, the alpha—Eila could only assume he was—lunged at Glisten, jaws snapping. She reared, barely avoiding the beast's razor-sharp fangs. Eila held on tight as the snowstrider stumbled before regaining her footing. She raised her hand instinctively, summoning an ice shield to block the next attack.

The alpha smashed into the barrier, snarling as the shield shattered into a dozen jagged pieces. The alpha's glowing yellow eyes fixed on Eila with a predator's intensity.

"Eila!" Grimrock yelled, yanking Blizzard to the side to avoid a similar fate. "Keep moving!"

The alpha danced around the group to herd them toward his pack. The beast leapt for Glisten's throat.

Eila conjured a blast of freezing wind and sent it into the alpha's face. The creature howled in fury, its frosted fur crackling. It landed on all fours, pawing his eye, then twisting back to Eila with renewed anger.

"Eila!" Corvus shouted desperately.

The ravenkin wobbled unsteadily on the snowstrider. He turned, face pale from exertion, and forced his hand forward to summon the shadows. Dark tendrils shot from the ground and wrapped around the alpha's legs. The beast snarled and thrashed, trying to break free, but the shadows held strong.

"Now!" Corvus managed weakly. "Let's go!" He sounded as though he might pass out, his energy visibly waning.

Grimrock yelled to spur Blizzard forward. Glisten obediently followed. They left the alpha behind since Corvus' magic continued to bind it, though he slumped as they rode on.

Wolves howled in a chorus as they emerged from the trees, the light brighter since the distance between boughs had increased. Eila crouched, urging Glisten on. They chased Blizzard out of the trees onto frozen tundra. Snow stretched in all directions, the wind biting as it swept across the plain.

"A little farther!" Grimrock warned.

Eila didn't need to ask why. She glanced over her shoulder, spotting the wolves as they burst from the tree line.

Eila's heart dropped since they showed no sign of slowing, and there were no more trees to arrest their speed.

She was about to call after Grimrock and Corvus when the wolves quieted. When she turned back, finding the wolves had gathered a short distance from the forest. There were at least twenty, eyes fixed on the escapees. As the snowstriders ran across the frozen ground, the wolves unleashed a bone-chilling howl.

As their howl reached its pitch, the alpha emerged. The beast paused beside his pack, then gave a frustrated howl that echoed across the frozen expanse. The pack did not follow them further.

Eila wondered how long their luck would hold, but there was still a job to be done. Tundra lay before them, and the open ground let the snowstriders increase the pace.

They were safe…

For now.

CHAPTER NINETEEN

The snowstriders didn't need Eila's encouragement. Spurred on by their encounter with the wolves, the striders quickly put distance between them and the mountains before exhaustion threatened to overtake them.

They slowed when rocks and hills took the place of the tundra. They briefly rested in a small cave, where Grimrock started a fire that kept Corvus' chill at bay. The ravenkin looked awful, skin still marked with black lines and heavy bags beneath his eyes.

Although his body was spent, it did not affect his humor. "We should tell those wolves, 'Fangs for a good run.'" He chuckled, but the sound turned into a cough.

All too soon they were back on the striders. Eila directed the creatures toward the cloud-blurred moon. Despite the blizzard, there was a big enough break in the clouds that Eila had managed to gain her bearing. They now raced toward the location she knew would be safe, a place only she and one other fae knew about. She was certain it would be unguarded.

As they got closer, they had to take cover when beating wings indicated Winter Court guards securing their perimeters. The additional activity was a nuisance, but Eila was pleased that they were heading in the right direction.

"Only a little farther," Eila commented, pointing at a large body of water, half-rimmed by sheer cliffs and frozen forest. On its surface were hundreds of dead fish. "That is Mirrormere, the lake of the reflection of the gods, a sacred place that harbors a secret."

She said no more before they reached the lake's edge. They skirted the water, heading toward the cliffs. Here the rock was smooth, as though the ice covering its surface had collected for centuries. Eila guided them to where a copse of trees and shrubs clung to a cliff, creating a hidden hollow between lake and rock.

There was a shift in the air as they approached the trees. Long shadows fell over them, and the biting cold deepened. She had not felt that for a long time, and she immediately felt young and small. Glisten stopped, and Eila hopped off.

Grimrock sharply scanned their surroundings. Corvus remained on Blizzard's back, slumped and snoozing.

"This place…" Grimrock muttered under his breath. "It is old."

Eila cocked an eyebrow. "How can you tell?"

Grimrock went to the ice-covered cliff and placed a palm on it. "I can feel it in the rock. It thrums in the air." He looked at Eila questioningly. "Where are we?"

"I don't know its official name," Eila replied. "I only know what Aria and I call it."

"Which is?" Grimrock asked.

"Coldwall Hollow," Eila replied. "I know, it's a shit name, but we were kids, so sue us."

Eila stood beside Grimrock, holding a hand up to the ice. She walked along its length, sliding her hand beside her as if looking for something. "We stumbled across it when we ran away. We were young and stupid and wanted to explore. We were sick of the palace and wanted to see the world."

"And you found your way here?" Grimrock replied. "Is this far from the palace?"

Eila pointed away from the wall. "The palace is a few klicks in that direction. On a clear day, you can actually see it."

She faced the wall, breath fogging. She looked away, disappointed, then continued walking and testing the ice with her hand.

"What led you here?" Grimrock asked, though he returned to Corvus in case the ravenkin fell off the snowstrider.

"I don't remember," Eila replied, though that wasn't true. She had a faint memory of running and giggling under a blazing sun that gave off no heat.

Aria was running ahead. Eila hunkered down and increased her pace, and when she pulled even with Aria, their feet tangled, and they fell. When she opened her eyes, a small light that whispered incomprehensible words was floating above her.

Eila had thought it was a butterfly, but when she rose and chased it, it became clear that wasn't the case. Aria followed, and before they knew where they were, they were facing the door.

A door that appeared in Eila's mind as she examined the blank cliff. "Where are you?" she whispered, trying to hold that memory in her mind. She stepped back, memories racing through her head. A flash of light illuminating the rock face and revealing the door, wards and runes carved into its surface, all appearing at a single word.

Eila leaned forward and pressed her head to the ice. She muttered the words that rose from her throat and was pleased when the light and the doorway appeared.

"Voilà!" Eila stepped back and motioned at the door.

"You learned French?" Grimrock asked.

Eila frowned. "What's French?"

She stepped back, admiring the intricate curves and patterns on the door. She gently nudged it, and the door swung back and revealed a tunnel a little taller than her.

"You'll have to duck," Eila informed Grimrock, who had bent to peer inside. She examined his width versus the tunnel's and added, "It might be a squeeze, too."

Grimrock grunted, adjusting his stance to maneuver into the tunnel. Corvus stirred on Blizzard's back, blinking when he saw the glowing doorway. "You found it?" His voice was raspy.

Eila shot Grimrock an uneasy glance. It would really be a squeeze with the troll carrying Corvus.

Grimrock helped Corvus off Blizzard's back. "Can you balance?"

Corvus' face indicated that he was in pain, but there was still life in him. Eila pulled his arm around her shoulder. "We'll take it slow, kiddo."

Before entering, she addressed the snowstriders, "Go. Eat. Hide. But stay close. We might need you again soon."

As if they understood, Glisten and Blizzard galloped away, skirting the icy cliffs, and disappeared.

"They were eager to leave," Corvus wheezed.

"Save your strength," Eila instructed, a soft smile on her face.

They entered the tunnel, Grimrock blocking the light. The door slammed shut, but the blue ice emitted its own light, guiding their way. Memories of years gone by flooded back, the pair so much smaller than she was now. The air was cold, and something thrummed around them—a magic she had never given a name to.

They went deeper, the air growing warmer as they descended. Grimrock tramped behind her, growling curses as he wrenched his body through the space, ice chipping off and falling around him. Corvus shuffled steadily, letting out a soft cough now and then. The tunnel seemed to stretch on endlessly.

"We're here," Eila stated.

The tunnel opened up, and Eila stepped into the heart of Coldwall Hollow. It was as breathtaking as she remembered.

Hidden beneath ice and rock, the cavern was a sanctuary of life and warmth, in cold contrast to the Winter Court.

The walls glittered with frost, but the floor was covered in vivid green grass and brightly colored flowers that would not survive the Winter Court's perpetual cold. Trees, thick with shimmering silver leaves, stood tall, their trunks twisting toward the glowing ceiling. From their branches hung fruit of all shapes and sizes, decorating them like ornaments.

In the center of the chamber was a well, its stone rim chipped and worn. Crystal-clear water trickled over its sides.

"Well, we found a new vacation spot," Corvus commented, his voice filled with awe as he bent to examine one of the vibrant flowers. Its petals were the deepest purple, and it radiated heat.

Grimrock frowned in confusion. "This…this should not be. How is this possible?"

Eila smiled. "I've asked myself that question many times. The Hollow defies everything we know about the Winter Court. It shouldn't exist, but here it is."

Corvus muttered, "Like you."

Grimrock stood by the well, flexing his shoulders since he was finally able to stand tall. He traced its worn edges. "There's magic here. Old magic. Powerful magic." He stared at Corvus. "Bring him here."

Eila guided Corvus to the well. Grimrock eased him down to sit with his back to the stone as a soft glow radiated from the stones. The troll cranked a handle, bringing up the wooden bucket, water leaking from the cracks and holes around its girth. He tipped the water onto Corvus' head.

Corvus gasped when water cold enough to raise goose pimples hit him. He tried to stand, but his legs gave out, and he turned wide eyes to Grimrock. "What the hell did you do that for?"

Grimrock examined Corvus. At first, Eila could only see the

ravenkin's discomfort, but then she noted the dark veins on his skin fading.

Eila nodded. "It's not the Crystal Pool, but it'll do. Only problem is, he's freezing, and his clothes are sodden."

Grimrock shrugged. "I took a gamble."

Corvus spoke through chattering teeth. "You a-a-a-ass-h-h-h-ho—" He shifted over to a patch of flowers, and their petals glowed brighter. He exhaled as warmth washed from their centers, making quick work of drying his clothes.

"Marvelous," Grimrock whispered.

Footsteps echoed from the tunnel.

They were silent as they all turned to face the tunnel. Eila grabbed at the Heart. Grimrock clenched his fists and planted his feet. Corvus remained seated but straightened his back, eyes locked on the tunnel's opening.

Grimrock stepped forward. "Be ready," he warned.

Eila's heart raced. Only Aria knew about this place, but they couldn't be too careful. With so many scouts out and about, she couldn't deny the possibility that Queen Amara's troops followed them here. For a moment she saw a band stalking through the tunnel to bring her back to the palace.

How could she explain why she had broken her banishment to a queen who had very little patience? Queen Amara was respected across the land, but she governed using her own rule book, and little swayed her opinion.

The air got colder. Shadows appeared: dark shapes with wings.

Eila's hands glowed brighter. "Steady," she whispered.

When the figures stepped into the light of the Hollow, Eila's breath caught.

"Eila!"

Aria Frostwing rushed forward, her face lit up with relief at the sight of her old friend. She was just as Eila remembered, white hair pulled back in a neat braid, frost tattoos in glittery patterns around her left eye. Being raised in the Winter Court had brought a harshness to her features, but that faded as her smile took over and she raced at Eila.

Eila's glowing hand fell as Aria pulled her into a embrace, and one word tumbled out. "Aria!"

"Thank the Mother, you're here!" Aria stated. "Lyrian told me about your intention to meet, but I didn't think I could to find this place again. It's been so many years."

"You remembered," Eila marveled.

"Of course I remembered," Aria returned. "How could I forget a place like this?"

Eila had many questions to ask, but she saw Lyrian over Aria's shoulder, his golden hair catching the mystic light in the chamber. His expression was stoic, his normal confidence tempered by the gravity of the situation.

"You have good friends," he told her. "Even in the harshest of courts."

Aria laughed and stepped back, allowing Eila to face her lover. As he grinned, his eyes darted to the Heart of Frostfire on Eila's chest.

"You found it?" Lyrian gasped. His eyes filled with wonder.

Eila nodded. "I told you I would. Surely you didn't think I'd fail?"

Lyrian shook his head. "Of course not, it's just... The guardian... I... Eila..." He ran toward Eila, stealing her breath as his lips warmed hers. Eila was so taken aback that she forgot the audience, who watched them with a mixture of reactions.

"I'd say, 'Get a room,' but we're in one," Corvus admonished, struggling to his feet. "When you're done with Eila, if I could ask for a favor, Summer Boy?"

Eila pulled away, lost for breath as she chuckled. "Would you do the honors? His coat got burned in the mountain."

Lyrian held out a glowing hand, and relief flooded Corvus' face.

"That's the shit," Corvus stated, his skin glowing with warmth.

"Don't make it weird," Lyrian returned.

"Says the boy who's starring in a porn flick," Corvus shot back.

Aria grinned. "Aren't you a fun bunch?"

Eila rolled her eyes. "Ignore them. Too much testosterone and not enough brain cells between them." She stood beside Aria, the pair studying Corvus and Lyrian.

Aria's gaze fixed on Corvus, and her eyes sparkled. "Why do I get the feeling that he has more brain cells than all of us combined?"

Corvus' cheeks flushed, and his gaze wandered to her frost tattoos. "Because smart sees smart," he replied, shifting into raven form to squawk before returning to human shape. "Ravens are the smartest birds."

"That's like saying dung beetles are the strongest insects," Lyrian chimed in. "I could still squash one with my boot."

The males glared at each other. Eila rolled her eyes. Aria grinned. "This is why we never allowed boys in our secret hideout."

"Speaking of," Corvus said, "what is this place? I've studied enough biology to know that those plants shouldn't grow without sunlight. And this well. Did someone live here before?"

Eila's gaze flicked to Grimrock, who was deep in thought, but she answered, "We don't know. I'm not sure anyone else knows about this place, either. I've never told anyone." She looked at Aria for confirmation.

"Me neither," Aria replied. "As for the plants, maybe science can't explain them, but magic can. You felt it too, didn't you? The energy that shifts when you enter this place. It's—"

"Revitalizing," Eila finished Aria's sentence.

"Man, there are two of them now." Corvus sighed. "I had just gotten used to one."

Eila's gaze lingered on Corvus longer than Lyrian was

comfortable with, so he cleared his throat and stepped closer to Eila. He wrapped an arm around her shoulder, eyes darting to the Heart before looking at the ravenkin. "This was a fun reunion, but I need to remind you how high the stakes are. The kingdom is falling into chaos, and the realms are under attack."

Aria turned to her friend. "It's Silas. He stole the Sceptre."

"I know," Eila replied. "It's okay, though. We know his plans. He's trying to gather magical items from each kingdom, but we won't let him. He can't do anything without this." Eila looked at the Heart, which could be mistaken for a simple pendant. Although it had become part of Eila, there was no pain.

"What *is* that?" Aria asked.

"The Heart of Frostfire," Grimrock replied. "The catalyst that sparks the Frostfire Convergence. Without this item, Silas can gather relics, but he will not succeed in his ultimate goal."

Aria's expression hardened. "I don't care about his ultimate goal. He has the Sceptre, and our kingdom is falling apart. We need to find him."

"It's not just your kingdom," Lyrian added, looking around. "My contacts reported that he also has the Verdant Crystal."

Corvus looked at Grimrock for explanation. "We went over this," Grimrock reminded him.

Corvus winced. "Forgive me; it's been quite the day. I'm not clear on the trinkets and gems."

"So much for brain cells," Lyrian muttered.

Grimrock continued, "The Verdant Crystal is the Spring Court's prize jewel. It is to the Spring as the Sceptre is to the Winter. That is grave news."

Eila ran a finger over the Heart. "At least Silas can't trigger another Cataclysm. That buys us time."

"Unless we find those items, the kingdoms will crumble," Aria stated. "Our people are already migrating to the Summer and Autumn Courts. Queen Amara is scouring the land, but no sign of Silas has been found. If he withholds the power of the Sceptre, we will be at his mercy. The other kingdoms can't accept us all, and without the magic of the everwinter, our people may die."

She stepped closer to Eila and took her hand. "It's not about the items anymore. We must find Silas before it's too late."

Mount the Crest of the Gods and face your true enemy. Where the peak is highest, an end will come. Whether it is good or ill is for you to decide.

Frostfang's words sang in Eila's mind. She looked at Corvus, who had the expression on his face he'd had when she left Agnes' house. There was something he wasn't telling her.

As Eila thought, the chill grew. "So, we'll find Silas and take the items back. If he doesn't have all four relics, he cannot trigger a Cataclysm. True?"

Grimrock nodded.

"He only has two," Lyrian reported, playing with his collar.

"If only that were true," someone said as a shadow darkened the opening.

Fenris entered, shrouded in layers of clothing and wraps, the tips of his fur spotted with snow and frost. He pushed back his hood, his bright yellow eyes like lamps in the hollow's gloom.

"Fenris?" Eila called as her eyes flashed to the crown atop his head. "What are you doing here? You're supposed to be hiding."

"I received your communications." He looked at Eila, then Aria. "You were foolish to take on so much alone. My operation—"

"Your operation doesn't understand this court," Eila retorted, needing to defend her actions. "I did what I believed was right." She pointed a finger at Fenris' chest. "I hoped you would stay in hiding. Your crown is one of the relics Silas needs to complete his plans, and you strolled straight into Faerie, where he can get at it."

She stepped closer. "If you really want to help, and you *truly* believe in your operation, go back to Nemora and do not leave until this is over!"

"*Eila!*" Fenris' eyes blazed and he seemed to double in size as he loomed over Eila. The sight was alarming enough that Grimrock and Lyrian drew closer to her. "You know not of what you speak," Fenris continued. She had believed he was a good guy, and the idea of bringing him down filled her with sadness. Her fingers flexed, and the Heart woke.

"The Crown is gone," Fenris stated. "The Autumn Court is vulnerable."

The words fell like lead, and silence followed. The group looked at each other like Fenris had gone mad.

Corvus broke it. "My mother used to do that with her glasses. She'd be, like, 'Every time I put my glasses in a safe place, I lose them.' I'd point to her head. 'They're right there, Mum.' She'd laugh, and I'd laugh, and Dad would roll his eyes."

Fenris was quiet.

"It's on your head," Corvus added, as though he were speaking to a toddler. "Right there."

Fenris' shoulders sank. "You misunderstand, feathered one. This is not *the* Harvest Crown."

Eila's brow wrinkled. "What do you mean, it's not *the* Harvest Crown?"

"Do you really think the Autumn Court would allow an exile to wear its token?" Fenris asked. "This is a replica, a token of gratitude I received a long time ago. It was imbued with new magic."

Aria waved her hands. "Wait. I'm new to this circle, but you all believed that guy was guarding *the* most powerful magical item the Autumn Court possesses? Where does he live?"

Eila looked at Grimrock for help.

Corvus shrugged. "In a pub in London."

"Pah!" Aria exclaimed in disbelief.

"Not all items have to remain near their charges to maintain their effects," Grimrock replied. "I suspected that might be the case, but tales and legends and the histories of the items are hard to come by. Each court operates by its own rules, so I believed Eila."

"*Shit!*" Eila laced her hands behind her back as the words echoed around the cavern. "Silas has *three* of the items he needs? He just needs the Summer Court's relic and the Heart, and he can conduct his ritual." She fondled the Heart as Frostfang stated, *Crest of the Gods... Your true enemy... An end will come.*

The Crest of the Gods. Every faerie in every kingdom had heard of the place. It was the central meeting point for the realms, a place where magic converged. From there, the citizens could portal to the other kingdoms, the doorway unguarded due to its isolated location.

Most faerie doors were in the palaces and or close to the court, but the Crest not only held the reservoirs of magical power for each kingdom, but which each race was warned against using its doorways because a powerful evil magical deity kept his gaze on the peak.

She saw Silas and his faerie bandits scaling the mountain, flying above the snow and the rocks and the ice to enter the Summer Court. The Summer Fae would be on high alert after hearing news of the fall of the three, and they would guard the doors, but would anyone suspect that Silas had betrayed his orders to take his chances on the Crest?

Eila's gaze dropped to the Heart. "I must find Silas."

Corvus scoffed. "That is obvious. Where will you…" His voice trailed away, and he had that knowing look in his eye again. He stumbled as he crossed to Eila. "No. It's too dangerous."

"What?" Aria asked. "What is she doing?"

Grimrock answered for Eila. "She's going to scale the Crest."

Eila cocked her head. "How do you…"

Grimrock interjected, "You think the dragon only projected to you? Even with your centuries in this realm, you are but a nymph."

Eila's cheeks flushed. Frostfang had also spoken to Grimrock. Was that also how Corvus knew?

"Dragon?" Aria gasped. "Would someone fill me in, please?"

"There's no time," Eila waved a hand. "If we want to stop Silas, we have to get ahead of him. If it's not too late." She clutched the Heart, finding its warm radiance reassuring. "This is a journey only for fae kin."

Grimrock stepped forward.

"Grim, no," Eila commanded. "You would need wings. Time is of the essence, and we cannot hold back." She glanced at Fenris. "You too, Fuzzface."

Fenris bristled.

"I'm coming," Corvus stated as Lyrian shifted. "You said those with wings, so I'm coming."

"You'll freeze before we get there," Eila stated. "Can't take the risk."

Corvus stepped close and put a hand on her shoulder. He glanced at Lyrian, then leaned to Eila's ear to whisper, "I don't trust him."

"That's not your call," Eila hissed back. "I do." She wrapped her arms around Corvus. "You are exhausted. Rest, and if we... *when* we return, you'll see that your mistrust was for nought."

Corvus seemed set to protest, but Eila turned to Lyrian. "Are you with me?"

"Always," Lyrian replied.

Aria shook her head. "Don't even think about it. I might be new to this party, but if you're heading into the frozen wilds to track Silas down, you're leaving these merry men in the lurch. I will shelter them. There's a place not far from here with a warm fire, food, and clean unburned or torn clothes. I will protect them until this is over. Are you with me, gentlemen?"

Grimrock, Corvus, and Fenris did not reply.

"Perfect. They're in," Aria stated.

Although Eila was unhappy about leaving the others behind,

it was the only way. She bade the group goodbye, pausing longer with Corvus than Grimrock, then she took Lyrian's hand.

"Are you ready to face the end of the world?" she asked.

"I'd have no other faerie by my side," Lyrian replied.

Aria gagged. "Get going. Time is of the essence."

Moments later, Eila took to the snowy sky, Lyrian's wings humming beside her.

She hoped that she wasn't making a mistake. That they would find Silas before the final chess move was made and the world crumbled around them.

CHAPTER TWENTY

Icy winds howled around them as Eila and Lyrian flew, their wings cutting through the air with precision.

Faerie stretched out below, a vast, cold wilderness full of ancient forests and snow-covered mountains. The once-familiar land of Eila's birth now felt foreign, as if the essence of the Winter Court had shifted, corrupted by the darkness that now plagued its people. Villages were empty. Farmland was fallow. On a typical flight over the kingdom, one would encounter other Winter Fae, but it was as though the world had already ended.

Snow and gusts buffeted them as they fought through the frozen sky. Built for the cold, Eila trundled onward, while Lyrian's Summer magic melted the snow before it reached his skin. He was like a shooting star, a beacon of hope that flew alongside her. She was glad he was by her side.

Occasionally, Eila spotted breaks in the writhing clouds and saw stars twinkling faintly. Once, she spotted the moon, full and bright. Jagged purple flashes snaked through the clouds like dragons, illuminating the peaks of the mountain range now below them, signaling the beginning of their climb. The skeletal branches of barren trees reached toward the sky like twisted claws.

Eila glanced at Lyrian. His brow was furrowed in concentration. There was no need to exchange words. Both knew the Crest of the Gods lay ahead, a place few ever visited.

They flew in silence, the rhythmic beats of their wings the only sounds in the vast emptiness of the winter night. The cold bit Eila's skin, but it wasn't the chill that unsettled her; it was the oppressive quiet that blanketed the land, as if the world were holding its breath.

She also couldn't shake the feeling that they were being watched. The shadows in the forests seemed to shift unnaturally, and every gust of wind carried a faint whisper, as though the land was warning them to turn back.

A ribbon of frozen water wound below them. After several hours, Eila signaled Lyrian to follow her as she descended. She landed in a dip between tall rocks where water had pooled and frozen.

"Why are we landing?" Lyrian asked, looking around as though he expected something to jump out at them. "We have some distance to go."

"We need to keep our strength up," Eila replied, moving toward some bushes that had appeared empty when they were airborne, but now displayed large black fruit camouflaged with the bracken. They fit in Eila's palm. "Silas hasn't killed everything yet."

Eila bit into the fruit, the skin yielding to her teeth. Deep purple liquid poured over her hands, sticky and sweet.

Lyrian watched the fruit juice stain the ice red. "It looks like it's bleeding."

"It's bleeding *delicious*," Eila quipped, winking at Lyrian. "London humor."

Lyrian laughed, the lines on his face softening and his eyes sparkling. Eila remembered why she was so attracted to him.

"London looks good on you," Lyrian commented. Eila's cheeks flushed. "I prefer Faerie Eila, though."

Eila wiped the fruit juice off her lips, struggling to hide her smile. Lyrian's gaze remained on her, and when she looked up, he beamed, warming the frigid air around them. For a moment, it was as though the world hadn't fallen apart and they weren't flying toward what might be the end.

She drew closer. "Here, try one. It'll boost your strength."

Lyrian took the fruit, but his expression faltered when he examined it. "It's not as appealing to the eye as the fruit in the Summer Court."

"You eat with your mouth, not your eyes," Eila returned.

Lyrian grinned. "Speak for yourself." He took a careful bite, his wings giving a faint flutter as the juice dripped down his chin.

"Well?" Eila asked.

"Not bad," Lyrian admitted, his voice muffled by the mouthful. "Not great, but not bad."

Eila chuckled and gazed at the rocky peaks surrounding them. Purple flashes were becoming more frequent, but Eila wasn't sure if it was because of their proximity to the Crest of the Gods or the lateness of the hour.

Across the lake was a single tree in bloom, unaltered by the crumbling power in the realm. Its branches drooped like a willow's over the lake's frozen surface. Eila remembered the days before London and the beauty of the kingdom she was fighting to save.

"Do you think they'll ever be the way they were?" she asked. "Our kingdoms?"

Lyrian moved his hand to his chest, fondling something through his shirt. Finally, he answered, "No."

Eila studied his face. She couldn't figure out if sadness or something else colored his cheeks. "What do you mean?"

Lyrian met Eila's gaze and returned to the present. "Are things ever the same after chaos? Silas might not have started the new Cataclysm yet, but hasn't this situation shone a light on the dangers of relying on things to continue in stasis? All those people gathered at the palace are scared and want change. I can't imagine this event will be forgotten for many generations."

He took a deep breath. "Should you be successful in stopping Silas, Queen Amara will be accountable for many things. Her protections failed, and Silas took the Sceptre. You can't come back from that."

Eila digested that. He was right. Though the worst had yet to happen, fear was a powerful catalyst, and this situation had revealed the vulnerabilities of a kingdom that relied on a single item for the majority of its power.

"Don't put all your eggs in one basket," her mother used to say.

Lyrian discarded the stone of the fruit on the snow. The drops of juice made it look like he had injured himself.

He put a hand on Eila's cheek, his palm warm as she leaned into it. "Nothing remains the same, Eila. You of all people should know that. Change happens, whether we want it to or not. Change is the only constant. The choice we now have is whether to grow from the change or shrink in its wake."

He motioned around. "These trees and bushes and the fish in this lake have all diminished under the weight of the change. That one tree and these fruits survived. Not just survived, but they got stronger. That's life. We live, we fight, and we survive." He shot a thoughtful look at the sky. "I don't think things will be the same after this, but good things will happen. You'll see."

Eila frowned. Lyrian's words did not provide the comfort she had hoped they would. He kissed her, pressing his body against her. His glow protected them both from the snow. Eila closed her eyes, transported back to the summer fete what felt like moons ago, his smell enveloping her senses.

She pulled him closer, and her tongue danced with his. For a beat, she wished she could be anywhere but here with Lyrian.

Life had once been simple, and with Lyrian by her side, she could hope it could be again.

Eila broke the kiss and rested her forehead on Lyrian's. Her heart thumped, and her cheeks were flushed. "If Silas isn't at the Crest, we could take a door to the Summer Court and finish this." She smirked. "Your home has yet to crumble."

Lyrian returned the grin. "I would love that." He took a deep breath and broke contact. "Unfortunately, we have a job to do."

Eila theatrically rolled her eyes. "Killjoy."

Lyrian opened his mouth to retort, but a flash of light pierced the sky.

Eila dove out of the way as a bolt of magic struck the ground where she'd been standing.

She looked at the clouds and saw a dozen faeries speeding toward them.

Corvus shifted uneasily on Blizzard's back, barely holding on. His mind was a tangled mess of exhaustion and worry. Grimrock held him tightly from behind.

Lyrian's heat had waned. The warmth that he had reveled in a short while ago was a distant memory. He focused on holding onto the snowstrider. An uneasy feeling settled over him as he stared into the blizzard, wondering about Eila. *I hope she's okay.*

Corvus glanced at Fenris, who looked regal as he rode Blizzard straight-backed. The druid, or werewolf, whatever the hell he was, was as watchful and stoic as normal. Aria hovered in front of the striders, flying just above the snow, her wings a blur against the gray sky.

The landscape shifted, farmland morphing into villages and rolling hills. Aria hadn't told them where her safe house was, but Corvus trusted her.

Any friend of Eila's is a friend of mine. Except...

Lyrian's green eyes appeared in his mind and transformed into the blue and red that had filled his vision.

Something's wrong. The air fizzed.

"Speak your mind." Grimrock rumbled. He was a steadying presence in the cold.

Corvus frowned. "It's Eila."

"Another vision?" Grimrock asked.

"No, it's just… Can't you feel it, Grim? We're waiting for the world to exhale."

Grimrock didn't answer. Corvus didn't know much about the ancient troll, but he could tell that Grimrock was uneasy.

"We should've gone with her," Corvus stated as trees whipped by. "We should've insisted."

"Eila was right," Grimrock returned. "Time is of the essence, and we do not possess her abilities."

"Grim!" Corvus rebuked.

"We cannot assist with this chapter in the story," Grimrock insisted. "Regardless of our desires, we must play our parts. I dislike this as much as you do. We will have roles to fulfill anon."

Corvus couldn't help but grin despite Grimrock's sour words. "You speak as though we're characters in a story. Eila said you were into writing, and that is right on the nose."

"Everyone is a character," Grimrock explained. "Every want or need is a story waiting to be written. I have lived a thousand chapters in my life, and I do not think this will be our end. Eila has great influence, and there is more to her than meets the eye. No matter the outcome of this arc, I believe more volumes will be written."

Corvus turned his head to see Grimrock. "You're hiding something."

Grimrock grinned. "The unknown makes the story exciting."

Before Corvus could respond, Aria called, "Only a few more miles."

Corvus returned his attention to the land, although his mind was filled with Grimrock's words. If this *was* a story, wouldn't the plot point to Eila's confrontation on the mountaintop? Perhaps he should have said something. He could have warned her about what he had seen.

He *had* to warn her.

As if the vision were summoned by his thoughts, it came again. The white world shifted, Blizzard's body melting as Corvus looked at the mountain's spine and saw Eila screaming, her hands radiating more power than Corvus had seen her wield as she faced her enemy. The other combatant's identity was hidden by the magical flash that lit the sky, forcing Corvus to shield his eyes.

A body lay on the ground beside the enemy, long silver hair trailing down its back as the monster of the skies returned and large black shadow wings parted the clouds and roared.

The magic reached its peak. Eila was blasted back, her screams reaching fever pitch. Corvus slumped, his head smacking into Grimrock's hard chest, then gasped, jerking back to reality. His chest heaved from the force of the vision. The world came rushing back, the cold air biting his skin, but he barely noticed. His heart raced, his pulse pounding in his ears.

Grimrock steadied him. "Corvus? What did you see?"

Corvus just looked at Grimrock. The troll sensed the thoughts running through his mind.

Grimrock nodded curtly. "We all have our part to play." He looked at the horizon, showing Corvus the way without a word. "Stay true. Do not let the wind blow you off-course."

Corvus nodded and took a deep breath, summoning the energy he'd need. With a final glance at Aria and Fenris, he slipped off Blizzard's back and smoothly shifted into raven form. His wings unfurled, black feathers rejecting the icy wind as he took to the air. The pull toward Eila was overwhelming, driving him forward with every beat of his wings. He couldn't waste another moment.

He had to reach her.

No matter what the elements threw at him, he had to warn her.

He did not want another death on his conscience.

Eila barely registered the oncoming faeries before another blast forced her to roll to the side and brace herself. She scrambled to her feet, wings flaring as she leapt into action. The fae soldiers sped toward them, dark silhouettes against the stormy sky. They wielded a dangerous, powerful magic that hummed with energy.

"Lyrian!" Eila called, her voice barely cutting through the howling wind. He was on his feet, wings unfurled and glowing. His face was hard and focused, but when his eyes met hers, she saw concern.

Then she saw *him*. Silas hovered behind the faeries, grim satisfaction on his face.

"Silas," Lyrian muttered, stepping closer to Eila. His hand glowed as he gathered power.

"What kind of coward hides behind kin?" Eila called, not hiding her anger.

"A smart one," Silas called back. "You will never understand. The mighty are not accountable to the weak, the dirty, or the *banished*."

He flew higher, laughing as he darted toward the peaks, leaving his soldiers behind. Eila wanted to follow, but several fae blocked their passage as Silas slipped into the blizzard.

"Shit," Eila muttered, her magic responding to the adrenaline flooding her veins. "We'll have to fight our way out." The Heart pulsed, its warmth soothing her. They could not avoid this fight if they wanted to stop Silas.

"I like a challenge." Lyrian shot a fireball at the faeries above him, but they parted, twisting to avoid his attack.

One of Silas' soldiers shot toward Eila like an arrow, magic crackling from her fingertips. Eila launched into the air and spun out of the way as a bolt of electricity ripped through the space she'd occupied seconds before. Eila sent a bolt of freezing magic at the faerie, but the soldier dodged it with ease.

Eila gritted her teeth, hands igniting with ice-blue energy as she cast a spell that confined the nearest soldier in a cage of frost. The Heart beat faster, its reassuring energy inundating her as she conjured the shield and the sword. The faerie struggled in her ice prison, thrashing and screeching in frustration.

Lyrian battled fiercely, flinging golden fire at his attackers. His movements were fluid and graceful despite the chaos. He wove through the enemy's ranks, his blasts never quite meeting their targets but disrupting their formation and keeping them on their toes.

"*Watch out!*" Eila shouted as a wave of magic sped toward him. Lyrian lurched, and the blast narrowly missed the side of his head.

Movement drew Eila's gaze to the right, and she interposed her shield to block the blow. The muscular fae was smug as he barreled toward her. She slashed at him, opening a wound across the faerie's chest that froze as he reeled out of the sky.

Lyrian dodged, then parried an attack with a concentrated beam of light. Another faerie came up behind him, wrapping his arm around the Summer Fae's neck. The soldier dragged Lyrian back, gurgling and struggling.

Eila pointed the tip of the sword at the faerie, and daggers flew from its tip. One buried itself in the faerie's side.

The enemy fae loosened his hold and Lyrian broke free, grunting in pain when another attack grazed his side. He remained airborne, but the damage was clear on his face.

Eila sped toward him, and they hovered back-to-back as they faced the throng.

"We can't take them all," Eila called, panting. They needed to retreat, find Silas, and reach the mountain's peak before he crossed into the final realm. "We have to move *now*!"

"Cover your eyes!" Lyrian whispered, his pain barely concealed. "This might sting a little."

Eila threw her arm in front of her face. Holding one hand above him, Lyrian cried out, and a blinding flare exploded from his palms like a thousand flashbulbs, stunning their attackers.

"Now!" Lyrian urged, grabbing Eila's hand and pulling her toward the peaks. Eila allowed herself to be led. The pair darted higher, wings pumping furiously as they shot toward the Crest.

Silas' soldiers blinked stupidly, pawing their eyes as they tried to find the pair.

"Fly like you've never flown before," Lyrian commanded. He glowed, providing Eila with the light she needed to follow him.

Eila obeyed, heart thumping as she remembered Silas' smug face. How could one faerie conjure such chaos? And what would happen if they were too late?

Eila shook her head. She couldn't ask those questions when so many lives were at stake.

CHAPTER TWENTY-ONE

"Keep pushing!" Eila called. The storm had intensified. They fought the unforgiving winds that howled through the craggy peaks that rose before them like the jagged teeth of a monstrous creature. Each gust felt like it could rip Eila from the sky, as though it was an enemy fighting on the side of Silas. The world was a swirling maelstrom of snow and crackling energy, and visibility was almost nil. She gritted her teeth, determination alone keeping her aloft.

The air was thick with magic, heavy and oppressive. *What is happening?* Eila squinted into the snow as she kept pace with Lyrian. *It's as though the mountain is reacting to our presence. Did Silas bring the items with him? Was the mountain sensing those?*

Eila's breath came in short gasps, each exhalation turning to frost. She glanced at Lyrian, who flew just ahead of her, glowing like a star. He looked back in concern, but they both knew what awaited them at on the Crest of the Gods.

Something flashed on the ground, and almost out of sight, dark shapes lingered. Eila didn't know if they were Silas' henchmen, but she zagged off-course.

Her Winter Fae resistance to the cold was wearing thin, and she had to fight the urge to pull her wings in and plummet to escape the relentless wind. Her arms were heavy, her magical energy flickering and struggling against the raw power of the storm, but she couldn't stop when they were so close.

"We're going to have to land soon!" Lyrian shouted, his voice nearly drowned by the roaring wind. "We can't fly much longer."

"We can't," Eila shot back. "But we're close."

"How do you know?" Lyrian called back.

"Can't you feel it?" A buffet of wind twisted her shoulder and turned her around. She fought to regain her balance as lightning exploded above them, turning the peaks purple. Thunder followed almost instantly, shaking the air like the growl of an ancient slumbering beast.

"There!" Eila called, her voice swept away by the wind as something caught her attention.

A short way ahead was the mountain's crest. Above the peak, a swirling whirlpool of clouds spun threateningly and purple power flashed around the ring. The center was dead calm, the clouds revealing the starry sky and the gleaming moon.

A faerie waited atop the mountain, arms stretched before an active door.

Anger coursed through Eila when she identified Silas standing proudly with the Icicle Sceptre in one hand. Eila fought through the storm toward the center, but when a powerful gust struck both Eila and Lyrian, they dropped.

"Not now," Eila bellowed as the rocky slope rose to greet her. She twisted upright, wings wide to catch the wind to slow her fall. Beside her, Lyrian caught himself and asked, "You okay?"

She gave a curt nod, determined. "Let's finish this."

They rose higher, Eila stretching every flight muscle to make it to the peak. Snow stung her eyes and the wind ripped at her wings, but moments later, they entered the eye of the storm. Eila almost fell from the sudden change.

Silas stood close to the Faerie Door. Eila flung ice daggers surged toward him. Silas waved a lazy hand without looking, melting the daggers.

Eila and Lyrian landed a short distance from the faerie. "Silas! Stop!" Eila commanded. "It's over. You're done."

Silas did not turn. Eila's hair stood on end, wondering if Silas had already passed through the door, and this was a copy. A substitute to trick Eila into believing she'd found her target.

Silas turned, and when his eyes locked onto Eila's, she gasped.

The storm was worse than Corvus had anticipated.

Each wingbeat was a battle. The icy wind chilled him to the bone. His raven form, though adept at navigating strong winds, struggled against the relentless onslaught of snow and ice. It gathered on his wings, and clung to his feathers, adding weight. The storm wasn't natural. It felt alive, as though the mountain was conjuring this tempest to keep him from reaching Eila.

He couldn't lose her. *Wouldn't* lose her.

*Come on...come on...come on...*Corvus kept his keen eyes fixed on the horizon. Mountains rose around him, and staying on target felt all but impossible since his vision was clouded by the swirling snow. Every gust threw him off-course. Though he trained his eyes on the sky, hoping for a glimpse of the moon and stars to guide him, there were only dark clouds and bolts of purple lightning.

Which way was he going? Had he flown too far west, or had he veered east, pushed by the heavy gusts?

More importantly, had that lightning been in the visions that had plagued his mind? Was he too late?

Corvus croaked in frustration, pushing his wings harder as he banked left. A while back, he had narrowly avoided faeries with magic on their fingertips and darkness in their hearts. A few he had followed, but they had landed because of the storm.

His heart pounded, hollow bones singing with cold. He had always trusted his instincts before, but in the freezing grip of this storm, his senses were betraying him. For all he knew, he could be flying in circles.

Stay true. Grimrock's voice echoed in his mind, steady and reassuring. But Grimrock wasn't here, and Corvus wasn't sure what "true" meant when the world was just snow and ice and rock.

The gusts threatened to tear him from the sky, and he flailed his wings, feathers catching the wind at the wrong angle. A chunk of snow hit his eye, blinding him on one side and affecting his flight. He spiraled down, trying to right himself.

Corvus crashed into snow so deep that it closed over his head. He fought to stand, struggling to stretch his wings in the drift, then morphed into human form, knee-deep in a snow so heavy and cold it felt like it was clutching his ankles with frosted fingers. He hopped, using the momentum to shift back to raven form, but he couldn't get any lift. He crashed back into the snow.

You'll never reach her in time.

The thought came unbidden. Corvus' heart beat hard, doubt worming its way through his mind like poison.

What if Eila was dead?

What if Silas had won?

The vision came again—Eila screaming, surrounded by light and darkness. The blast of power that knocked her back. It repeated, gnawing at him. He attempted to fly again.

He crashed again, accepting the cold and letting it flood his body. He croaked, a desperate sound that was swallowed by the wind. He beat his wings hard in a last-ditch attempt to become airborne that drained his energy.

Impossibly, he caught the wind. He beat his wings furiously

and gained height, excitement and adrenaline rushing through his body as lightning flashed overhead.

He could do this. He would help Eila.

A wild gust jerked him off-balance, and he dropped like a stone, exhausted. He slammed into a rock and rolled to the ground, disappearing into the snow for the second time.

Eila...

With a final push, he shifted to human form, breathless and frozen. His black clothes and dark hair stood out against the white, but snow piled on top of him, camouflaging his body. He didn't shiver. He had no energy for that. His eyelids fluttered as dark shapes swirled in the snow and he thought of Eila, Grimrock, and his brothers and family. Would they be proud of his efforts? Would anyone tell the story of Corvus' last flight?

Would his body be found? He hoped so. As darkness closed around him and his lips turned blue, Corvus' final thought was his regret that he hadn't warned Eila.

Silas' eyes were crystal-blue: no black pupils, no white sclera, just light that radiated from where the pupils should have been.

"Eila," Silas crooned. As his gaze locked onto hers, Eila spotted the Harvest Crown atop his head, its tangles of thorns and berries identical to Fenris' headwear. In his hand, the Icicle Sceptre thrummed with power, and the Verdant Crystal hung around his neck, gleaming from its proximity to the other items.

Worst was the confident grin on his pale face. Anger boiled in Eila's gut as she recalled her last encounter with him in the throne room as he reveled in her expulsion from this kingdom.

"Naughty, naughty," Silas told her, voice low and menacing. "You shouldn't be here, Eila. You know better than that. You were *banished*."

She hated the way Silas' lips pursed as he wielded the word like a weapon.

"You know better than to take the Sceptre out of the palace," Eila shot back. "You won't be able to control what you're trying to unleash. No one can control the Cataclysm. No one will triumph when the worlds collide and fall into corruption."

Silas' grin didn't waver. "You really don't see it, do you? The future I envision. As the possessor of the relics, I will have the power to control not only this kingdom, but every faerie realm."

The Heart beat against Eila's chest. "Why?" Eila asked, trying to find any mote of compassion that might still exist in Silas' frozen heart. "Why are you doing all of this? You had power. You were in the queen's court, and you had influence. This?" She gestured at the swirling vortex. "This isn't power. This is madness. This is *chaos*."

Silas just stared at Eila.

His smirk grated on her. She took a step forward, the Heart beating faster against her chest. "Please, you don't need to do this. Give it up, Silas. End it now. If you go through that door, it won't be me that stops you, but the whole Summer Court. You think those guys won't guard their treasure with every defense they have after seeing all you've done here? You don't stand a chance. Stop before it's too late."

Silas stood straighter, teeth white in his wide smile as his haunting eyes glowed blue. "Oh, Eila. I feel for you, I really do. All your life, you've been subjected to the worst of my attentions, tarnished by a brush you would never understand, the grain of sand buried in my shoes all of these years, and you don't know why, do you?"

Eila was silent, hoping that Silas would deliver a nugget of information that might be useful to his downfall. As he spoke, she brought her power to the surface.

"You are a pawn, sweet girl," Silas continued as a thunder rumbled above. "You are a consequence of a larger game, and it is a shame that you will die without knowing what you are and what you could become. Your mother knows that. She has always known what is best for her darling baby."

Eila clenched her teeth and fists.

"Did I hit a nerve?" Silas asked.

"You keep my mother's name off your lips," Eila warned. "Do not tarnish her memory. She always knew what was best for me."

"Knows," Silas corrected, eyes sparkling.

Eila flinched, the word hitting her like a brick.

Silas pressed on. "You are correct, though. The Summer Court would line up all its defenses were I to step through that door. You can only bleed into the water so much before the sharks come. That's why I had to be subtle to get you here."

Eila mind burned with questions, but she was silent.

Silas' eyes narrowed. "We are a secretive breed, aren't we, Snowshadow? A court that revolves around deception and trickery and politics and manipulation. I was cunning enough to attain all four items for the Convergence *and* summon an enemy of this realm to deliver the catalyst into my hands." He stared hungrily at the Heart of Frostfire. "Now the ritual shall be complete."

Eila stepped back. "Wrong!" She grinned. "You don't have all four relics, Silas! The snow must have frozen your…"

Eila's words trailed off. During the interchange, she had almost forgotten about the faerie standing beside her. The faerie who, as realization dropped like a penny into a well, stepped closer to Silas, his long, familiar fingers digging under the collar of his shirt as he drew a pendant out from under his shirt—a gem in the shape of a runic sun, glowing bright orange as it reacted to his touch.

Lyrian stood beside Silas, eyes cold as he lifted his chin and removed the chain. He passed the Sunfire Amulet to Silas, then folded his arms.

Silas had triumphant venom in his voice when he spoke again.

"We already have them, Eila. The four relics of the fae courts. Now, all I need is that Heart."

A tear welled and rolled down to freeze on her cheek as the floor fell out from beneath her.

Lyrian just stared blankly at her.

CHAPTER TWENTY-TWO

"No."

The word was barely audible. Her mouth was dry, tongue sticking to the roof as she fought to understand what was happening. She shook her head but returned Lyrian's gaze, willing him to tell her this was a cruel joke.

Time slowed. The clouds swirled threateningly overhead as Silas laughed, placing the Sunfire Amulet around his neck. With the four items in his clutches, all he needed was the Heart to activate the Frostfire Convergence.

It nestled against her sternum. Reality crashed on her. It had always been Lyrian. It was clear now. How could she have been so blind?

"I see the pieces are falling into place," Silas crooned. Lyrian shifted uneasily beside him. "It's in the last move that the plan becomes apparent, isn't it? Lyrian has been my willing accomplice since Day One, and you fell for everything, hook, line, and sinker."

Eila tried to speak but couldn't.

"I thought it was going to be over after the commotion in the palace. Feels like that was many moons ago, doesn't it? The night your boyfriend was captured." He placed a hand on Lyrian's shoulder. "You've been an admirable fall guy, and an even greater companion. We had been trying to break into the vault to take the Sceptre, and it was *Lyrian's* idea to take the fall. He needed no encouragement because... What was it you said?"

"Eila would come," Lyrian's gaze flickered to Eila, a shadow falling over his brow.

"And Eila did come!" Silas exclaimed. "Gave into those feelings brewing in your chest. Helped Lyrian escape and let me send you far from this realm's walls. How has the mortal realm treated you, Eila?"

It was a rhetorical question, but she wanted to reply. She just couldn't. The Heart thudded against her chest, radiating a warmth through her that only rage could fuel.

"With Lyrian taking the fall and you paying the price, it took the heat off me. Easier to blame the Summer Court faerie than point the finger at me. Then it just came down to collecting the items. It's amazing how many faeries are willing to comply with your instructions when you manipulate their minds and point out the corruption already at work within our system. So many fae want change, and they are willing to work for anyone who represents change, no matter the cost."

"It... It was all..." Eila tried.

"Planned?" Silas replied. "Yes, it was, and your boyfriend was the key to it all. The rest of the fae kingdoms are weak. With the right people whispering the right words to the Autumn and Spring Courts, it was only a matter of waiting for the items to fall into my lap. And Summer? Well, I recruited the Summer champion to collect the last relic."

Eila turned her attention to Lyrian. "You lied. You told me the relic was safe."

"It was," Lyrian replied. "Corvus asked if the champion still had the relic." He sneered. "And I told you it was."

"Do your people know—" Eila started.

Silas interjected. "Lyrian is a master of deception. I've asked on many occasions if there isn't some Winter Court blood in him. *Something* had to attract you to him, Eila. You wouldn't just fall for anyone."

Hot tears welled in Eila's eyes. Her skin felt tight, and she wished the ground would swallow her whole. It wasn't just the betrayal and the deceit, but the embarrassment for not seeing through Lyrian's disguise. Corvus and Grimrock had warned her, but she had continued to believe it wasn't Lyrian. No wonder the Winter Fae froze their hearts and denied their feelings. Life was easier without them.

"It was *you*," Eila accused Lyrian, demanding his attention again. "In the Faerie Door with Maevis."

Lyrian shrugged as though Eila had just asked him where the salt was.

"To his credit, no. That was me." Silas smirked. "He's quite the thespian, but he has his limits. Still, he did manage to point you to the Heart of Frostfire. I wasn't sure you would complete the task, but here you are."

"I told you she was special," Lyrian stated, the words like daggers in Eila's heart. He had said those words under a summer sun, fresh from a fete.

Silas studied Eila. "You were right, and you led her here. Now we have it all, so we can begin the ritual."

Eila's heart thumped—not the jeweled one, but hers. All the items needed for the Frostfire Convergence were here.

But Silas did not have them all.

Eila took a step back as Frostfang's voice rang in her mind. *Mount the Crest of the Gods and face your true enemy. Where the peak is highest, an end will come. Whether it is good or ill is for you to decide.*

Silas' sneer dropped when he sensed Eila's plan. "It's no use. The wind will stop you, and if it doesn't, my men will find you. Hand me the Heart or die."

Eila gritted her teeth, preparing to spring. "I would rather die than contribute to the destruction of this world. You cannot control the future you envision, Silas. No one can. You will become a pawn in the hands of the gods of chaos, and where will that leave us all?"

"You know not of what you speak," Silas stated, planting his feet as the Icicle Sceptre glowed.

All three were silent, each waiting for the others to make the first move. Lyrian faced Eila. She wondered what he was truly capable of. Would he turn his powers on her? Their love had felt real. Surely it couldn't have been one-sided. There had to be something between them. Lyrian could not be what Silas said he was.

Lyrian's eyes twinkled with affection. Would it be enough to save her?

Eila lifted her chin. "Fuck you." The shield and sword appeared as the power of the Heart coursed through her. She leapt back and fired a beam of ice projecting from the sword's tip at the ground around Silas and Lyrian.

Silas roared as he pointed the Sceptre, waving away Eila's beam. Hailstones shot toward her. Eila raised the shield, and the hailstones sounded like bullets when they slammed into the ice.

Lyrian flew toward her, taking advantage of Eila's limited vision from behind the shield, as she re-entered the storm, determined to put distance between her and the others.

Snow pelted her, and the wind beat her body. Eila growled as she drew on her reserves to escape the peak. If she could find a place to put the Heart that they would never find, maybe the world would be saved, and the Convergence would only exist in Grimrock's books.

Her wings strained, and her breath came in ragged gasps. The air got colder and sharper the higher she climbed, the storm like a wall of fury. "You can do this, Eila. They cannot win," she muttered, the words torn away by the wind. She tried to silence the voice in her mind that whispered it was hopeless. Silas was too powerful. Lyrian's betrayal had cut too deep. She couldn't think about that. Not now. The mission was all that mattered. She had to protect the Heart.

As she gained height, a searing heat flashed behind her, and the air shifted unnaturally. She flinched as an invisible force yanked her back, spinning her through the air like a rag doll. She struggled to regain control, flapping her wings desperately to stabilize herself. She looked over her shoulder, flying directly toward her was Lyrian.

His eyes blazed with golden light, and his hands glowing with fiery magic as he closed the distance between them. Eila's heart clenched. The faerie she had loved and trusted was trying to capture her. For a moment, she hoped she could break through whatever spell Silas had placed on him.

"*Lyrian, don't!*" Eila shouted hoarsely. "You know what I have to do!"

Lyrian's expression was cold and distant, as if the bond they had shared had never existed. His gaze flickered to her chest, where the Heart pulsed with an icy glow. His jaw tightened.

"You know what I have to do, Eila." he said, his voice firm but edged with some deep emotion. Regret? Guilt? She couldn't tell.

Lyrian shot toward her, magic crackling around him like fire. Eila darted to the side, narrowly avoiding his grasping hands. Her heart screamed for her to fight, but she hesitated. This was Lyrian. *Her* Lyrian. How could she hurt him?

There was no time to dwell on the dilemma. Lyrian lunged at her, and Eila barely summoned a wall of ice to block his advance. The barrier shattered, and a vine snaked toward her, then wrapped around her wrists.

Eila tried to pull free, but the vine's grip was like iron. Eila sent a freezing chill into the vine, and it froze and turned black, but it held firm around her wrist.

Lyrian's eyes locked onto hers. She saw pain in his gaze, as if he, too, hated what he was doing. The moment passed, and his expression hardened. "I'm sorry, Eila," he whispered, his voice barely audible through the storm. He pulled her toward him and clutched her tight against his chest, magic flaring around them both.

The Heart raced and swelled, almost incandescent now, stinging Eila's eyes. She struggled, fists pounding Lyrian's chest, but he dragged her back toward Silas.

"*No!*" Eila shouted, her voice cracking with desperation.

Lyrian seemed unnaturally strong, and light limned his head. Eila's vision blurred with tears of rage and betrayal, her heart breaking anew. He unceremoniously dropped Eila on the ground, and the light around his head faded. Eila spat out snow as she got to her knees, staring up at Silas.

"As much as I enjoy watching your pain, my patience has expired." Silas pointed the Icicle Sceptre at Eila. "Lyrian, would you do the honors?"

Lyrian crouched beside her, gaze glued to the Heart, eyes wide and dreamy. Despite her protestations, he yanked it free, holding the glowing, beating relic in the palm of his hand.

"Now, Lyrian," Silas crooned, his platinum hair billowing behind him as the storm swelled.

Lyrian paused, and Eila saw a mischievous twinkle in his eyes before he walked over to Silas. His strides were slow, and when he reached the faerie, he dropped to one knee and presented the Heart like he was presenting a gift to a king.

Silas smiled, teeth bared. "At last!" The other relics glowed and pulsed. "Finally, the dawning of a new era in which fae can live without restrictions, and the worlds will bow to our power!" He laughed maniacally as he reached for the Heart of Frostfire.

The item rose from Lyrian's palm and raced past Silas' outstretched hand to his chest. It locked into place, beating frantically as Silas' excitement boiled over. He adjusted the Harvest Crown, and tightened his grip on the Icicle Sceptre. He placed the other hand on the Sunfire Amulet and the Verdant Crystal, and the light he gave off stung Eila's eyes and made thunder roll.

Silas' mouth hung open, though it didn't move. When he spoke, it was as though a dozen voices spoke at once: *"Expergiscimini antiquae copiae, hanc ianuam effringite."*

Eila sat back, fear piercing her heart as purple light gathered above them, almost as bright as the sun. Her skin broke out in goosebumps.

Lyrian watched stoically from beside Silas.

"And now, we open the door," the chorus bellowed as he raised his hand to the sky. Power shot from the tip of the Sceptre and snaked into the orb, white light melding with purple light. A bolt left the orb and pierced Silas.

Silas cried out so loudly that Eila would hear his pain for the rest of her life. She would also remember Silas' broken corpse half-buried in the snow, the items of power scattered around him.

CHAPTER TWENTY-THREE

Corvus groaned. His body was numb.

Surprisingly, it wasn't the flashes of light that brought him back to the land of the living. Corvus had only seen those from behind closed eyelids, the light show creating muted patterns in his fading mind.

Corvus had also seen his years in the human realm rushing by. He had seen his mother and father, proud civilians making a life for their children. He had seen their smiles and their love, as well as his pain during the funerals. He had seen his brothers Oscar, Logan, and Joshua running around and causing havoc as an exhausted Hayley watched them.

He had seen Eila and Grimrock, whose friendship was more of a surprise than anything else that had happened in his life. Ravenkin, banished and cursed, didn't make friends. But Eila had understood his plight. She knew what it was to be outcast. Grimrock, too. For years, the loveable hunk of rock had lived by himself. He knew not only the pain of isolation but also the joy of simple living.

Then the light show danced and exploded, raining power and magic on him. Corvus was rose as if huge hands had scooped him up out of the snow. As he was placed on a soft bed, he heard an animal snort.

He grinned as something warm covered him. Then, the world turned black.

The storm still swirled, but Eila and Lyrian were alone in the eye.

Eila stared at the burned body, which looked so small.

She could not see the Heart. Was it beating beneath Silas?

"What happened?" Eila asked. It seemed absurd to ask Lyrian like he was still on her team.

The other fae was calm, as if nothing unusual had occurred. Eila glanced at Silas, wondering if this was one of the stages of the ritual. Perhaps Silas would rise and glow, the power coursing through him as the Frostfire Convergence began.

But Silas was dead.

Lyrian walked over to Silas. "You wouldn't understand. He didn't either." He circled the body with hunger in his eyes. Eila tensed; she had to collect at least one of the items before Lyrian could. Then no harm would befall anyone else.

Eila stepped forward, and the air rippled as the heat washed over her. She gasped and checked for damage, but she was unhurt.

"That was a warning," Lyrian stated, bending down. He picked the Verdant Crystal, turning it over in his hands. "Beautiful items with an even more beautiful purpose." He spoke to himself. "I was right. It was meant to be."

"Lyrian," Eila demanded, taking a step forward. He flung a fireball at her. She swatted it away, ready now. "Leave the items. It's over. You're no longer under his influence, so you can leave this place. Return the items and restore the balance. Then we can go back to how things were."

Lyrian smirked, unable to tear his gaze away from the relics as he placed the Harvest Crown atop his head. "You still don't understand. It was never about Silas. He was just a stepping stone to the goal."

He placed the Sunfire Amulet around his neck as he reached for the Icicle Sceptre, whose handle was buried in the snow. "Silas wasn't the mastermind. He could never channel the Convergence. Don't you get it? One faerie cannot channel the power. The Convergence requires two.

"It's about pairing opposites and harnessing the energy that sits between realms. You must marry heat and frost. It's the Frostfire Convergence. Frost and fire can only be joined by the marriage of flame and snow. Summer and Winter."

Eila's heart dropped into her stomach, and a chill ran through her body. Lyrian gazed at her with that powerful want she had mistaken for lust. She now realized it was his thirst for the power and potential she represented. She had been played, as Silas had been played, and now she would be sacrificed in one of the most dangerous rituals the realms had ever seen.

"You can't," Eila began, her words more confident than she felt. She took a step back. "I won't let you."

Lyrian jabbed the Sceptre at her, and a block of ice formed at her back, preventing her from escaping.

Panic set in, and she leapt into the air. Before she got far, a light that shone from above blinded her, and brambles wrapped around her ankles and yanked her back to the ground. She landed on a bed of orange and brown leaves, and daisies and buttercups blossomed around her.

"The four courts are at my disposal," Lyrian commented, deadly calm. "You cannot fight me. Only give in."

Eila had taken Lyrian with her to the mountain, leaving Grimrock, Corvus, and the others behind to make better time. Now she was at his disposal. Blood rushed to her head, a low *whump-whump* that shooed her thoughts away. She glanced at the stoic face of her former lover as the sound intensified.

Whump-whump, whump-whump, whump-whump.

"Let's finish this. Stand with me as I open the gate. We can rule as king and queen. You can have the influence you've always wanted. The influence your mother fought for."

"Don't talk about her," Eila spat. She shook her head to clear the *whumps*, and her gaze went to Silas' corpse. A gentle glow pulsed beneath him. Words whispered into Eila's head: *A heart of ice and a heart of flame, a weapon to wield in the master's grand game. Two forces for evil, two weapons for kind, a power that will corrupt the mind.*

Two weapons? Eila realized that while Lyrian had the relics, he hadn't sought the Heart. Didn't he need the catalyst to complete the union?

Eila sprang to her feet and used her power to freeze the brambles. Before Lyrian could react, Eila kicked them, and they shattered. She raised a hand toward Silas's body. He juddered and jerked.

Lyrian frowned but made no attempt to stop her as the light beneath Silas' body got brighter. He rolled onto his back, revealing a pale face with blood on his lips. The Heart flew toward Eila's hand, and she caught the glowing jewel and placed it against her chest. The Heart breathed life and power into her body, and warmth spread around her.

Eila called up the shield and the sword.

Lyrian cocked his head. "It seems the Heart is ready. My turn. Are you prepared to unite, Eila?"

"Burn in the Iron Wastes," Eila replied, seething.

"This *will* happen," Lyrian stated. "Willing or no. Don't make me hurt you."

"You cannot burn a frozen heart," Eila returned, planting her feet he flung his magic at her.

Corvus huddled beneath the blanket. Warmth slowly radiated through his bones, thawing the chill. He tested his frozen fingers, and the bones complained. The stink of an animal rose from beneath him. "What the…"

He peeked out from under the blanket to see a stony hulk before him. "Grim?"

He shifted the blanket and saw Grimrock's back as he doggedly rode Blizzard up the mountain. The world whizzed past, snow pelting them as Blizzard trod an impossibly smooth path across the rocks and chasms they traversed.

"Grim?" Corvus called, louder this time.

"Hold tight, little raven," Grimrock instructed over his shoulder. "Your fight is not yet done."

Joy coursed through Corvus, a stronger heat source than the blanket, which he realized must be Agnes' cloak, and Blizzard's body. Relief mixed with his delight, and his eyes opened wider. "You found me!"

"I did," Grimrock replied. "Specifically, Blizzard found you. Must have been your stink. These beasts are keen trackers."

Corvus wanted to laugh, but his cheeks hurt. "Eila?"

"We'll save her if we can," Grimrock responded. "I only hope we're not too late."

Corvus shifted. A huge hand pressed gently pressed him down. "Rest. Save your strength for the fight ahead."

Corvus obeyed, his body listening though his mind didn't want to. Overhead, thunder clapped as lightning zagged, the storm loud enough to obscure Grimrock's whispered words.

"It might be the final fight for us all."

Lyrian's fire was a blinding sheet of heat and light. Eila raised her ice shield, and the Heart of Frostfire thrummed against her chest. The sheet crashed into the shield, and the edges melted.

"Enough games," Eila shouted over through the roar of the flames. "Let's end this."

Lyrian's smirk widened as he stepped forward, the Sunfire Amulet glowing brighter with every step. His wings cast an ethereal light through the storm. "It's just beginning." He summoned the wind. Eila's wings strained, and her feet slid across the snow as she struggled to maintain her balance.

Eila's gaze was cold as she drew on her power, amplified by the Heart. She darted forward, wings propelling her faster than the eye could track, and swung the sword in a wide arc, her emotional ties with Lyrian abandoned.

Lyrian summoned a barrier of green vines from the ground, thick and impenetrable as they writhed.

"Spring's gift," Lyrian declared, stepping around the wriggling vines, then stretched out a hand. More vines coiled around her legs and pulled her to the ground.

Eila grunted as she slammed into the snow, the impact knocking the air out of her lungs. She struggled against the vines, but they tightened their hold, thorns pricking her skin. She focused the Heart's power and sent freezing energy through the vines. They jerked and turned brittle, and a single slash cut them off.

She jumped to her feet, but Lyrian was waiting. An autumnal wind blew, carrying leaves so thin and dry that they were razor-sharp, and clipped her before she could raise the shield. Several leaves notched her wings.

Eila yelped, her skin stinging as blood dripped on the snow.

"Autumn's gift," Lyrian explained.

Eila struggled to catch her breath, her body aching from the relentless onslaught. Her strength waned, the fight taking its toll, but then a new determination burned in her chest. She would not let him win. She would not allow the Convergence to take place.

Lyrian smirked.

Eila's wings beat furiously as she shot toward Lyrian. Being injured, they didn't quite work right, and she fought to maintain her course.

Lyrian's eyes widened. Eila spun in midair, her sword glowing ice-white, and slashed at Lyrian's chest.

He caught the blade with his hand, his eyes burning with fury. "Winter's gift," he growled, and she realized his hand was covered in ice. He ripped the sword from Eila's grasp and flung it away. The sword vanished when it touched the snow.

Eila landed beside Lyrian, conjured the sword back into her hand, and slashed again, but thick ice guarded the soft flesh of his neck.

"It must hurt to see your kingdom leveraged against you," Lyrian mocked as heat radiated from his hands. "Now, experience Summer's gift."

Eila screamed when fire engulfed her, the searing pain overwhelming. She tried to maintain her position as flames poured over her. The Heart of Frostfire pounded her chest, making Eila wonder if it would shatter.

Then the fire was gone. Eila opened her eyes. She was standing in a large circle of gray stone filled with water. Lyrian stood a short distance away, that smile on his face as the Sunfire Amulet's light dimmed.

"Impressive." Lyrian nodded at her. "I didn't expect the Heart's protective wards to be so...powerful."

When Eila glanced down, ice covered her from neck to toe, reminding her of the medieval suits of armor she'd seen in London's museums. Inside the ice, the Heart still beat.

"Activated the moment the Heart met the relics' power," Lyrian informed her. "You think I'd kill you when we could rule together? This is merely a glimpse of what we could achieve. With ice and fire combined, we could be more powerful than any king and queen the world has ever known." His gaze took on a warmth that caught Eila off-guard. "Please. We can finally be together. Join me."

Eila's lips thinned. After everything Lyrian had done and the lies he had told, she could still feel his pull. Did the other realms have to deal with emotions casting their votes before they could take action? Eila had lived with the emotionless stoics of the Winter Court for centuries, never feeling a flutter of emotion, and now she was considering joining Lyrian.

"Answer one question first." Lightning flashed above Eila.

"Anything." Lyrian raised his chin, and the coldness returned to his eyes.

"Why me?" Eila asked. "You plucked me from the herd, and you played me. It could have been any faerie, but you chose me. Why?"

Lyrian sighed. "You really have no idea? Did Silas know more about your ancestry than you do?" He cocked his head like a bird assessing a worm. "Come with me and I will show you. Unite with me on this peak, and the answers will be yours." Lyrian held out a hand, the relics glowing brightly on his body. "The choice is yours."

The Heart beat rapidly under Eila's ice. She took an involuntary step toward Lyrian, experiencing a magnetic pull that got stronger as Eila fought it.

The storm roared.

"That's it, Eila. Give yourself to it. Allow the power to take you." Lyrian shifted, waiting expectantly.

Energy coursed through Eila's veins, and her tiredness and fatigue faded. The ice armor, though thick, allowed her to bend and move as though she wore nothing. She took another step, and the relics glowed even brighter.

"Yes," Lyrian crooned.

Another step, and Eila's body filled with static. She fixed her gaze on Lyrian as the power built inside of her, the Heart racing. Time slowed, and the mountain and the storm disappeared. Lyrian was replaced by her mother and father standing in their chamber at the palace. She saw them laughing and smiling, something they only did when they were alone in their quarters.

Her mother faded and her father's mirth turned to tears. Then they stood at Lysandra's graveside, the casket empty, symbolic but unsatisfying. She saw her father age rapidly and Aria beaming as they ran toward the Summer Fete.

She saw the queen's eyes boring into hers as the word "banished" left her lips, and a dirty underpass in a realm she had never entered. She thought about Thrumble, Harley, and Finn attacking Corvus. She felt her friend's embrace and smelled his scent and saw his smile. She saw Grimrock and heard the thunder produced by his custom typewriter.

The people and the memories she cherished would be erased if she didn't defeat Lyrian, but the relics' power was compelling.

Love infused her power, and her palms shone brighter than the relics he wore. The resulting flash hurt Eila's eyes.

Lyrian cried out.

A raven screeched.

CHAPTER TWENTY-FOUR

Eila stumbled back and landed badly, but leapt back to her feet. The light faded to reveal Lyrian on one knee, panting. His head snapped up, eyes glowing with power akin to Silas' as his lips curled. He laughed. "You made your decision. So be it." He raised his hands.

Eila gasped. Dark tendrils sprang from the ground and coiled around Lyrian's wrists and ankles. His spell misfired, scorching the ground beside Eila.

A squawk got Eila's attention as a raven landed beside her. Corvus staggered, then fell to one knee.

"Corvus!" Eila exclaimed, her excitement mingled with fear at his state. His veins were ink-black, the corruption from his cursed magic almost total. She didn't know how much more he could take. "What in the Iron Wastes are you doing here?" Her gaze flicked to Lyrian, who was fighting the tendrils. "You should be resting. You can't be here now."

"Rest?" Corvus let out a hollow chuckle. "It's hard to rest when the world is crumbling and the monsters have broken loose." He looked up at Eila, pain and admiration glinting in his tired eyes. "Besides, you need us."

"Us?"

Grimrock came into view, looking larger and more determined than she had ever seen him. With each bound, he covered several feet. She had never seen him move so quickly. Where had he hidden that agility?

"*Grim!*" Eila shouted.

Corvus groaned and stretched his arms out as Lyrian gained traction over Corvus' magic. The more the evil fae fought, the more the ravenkin hunched his back and slumped.

"Enough!" Eila called.

Grimrock reached them. She started to address him, but Grimrock barreled at Lyrian, clenching his fists on the descent. As his fist connected with Lyrian's head, a flash of light deflected his move, and the troll skidded back.

Between Grimrock's attack and Corvus' diminishing power, her relief at their arrival was quickly morphing to concern.

"Eila," Corvus managed. "*Go!*"

Eila summoned the sword and the shield and raced toward Lyrian. She slashed at her former lover, though Lyrian's magic created a shield. It was not strong enough to block Eila's fury. The sword opened a wound on Lyrian's bicep that gushed blood down his arm.

Lyrian hissed, and his muscles coiled as he unleashed his power. The shadow tendrils burst into flame and retracted into the ground. Corvus dropped to his hands and knees.

"*Grim, now!*" Eila shouted and was pleased to hear the troll's thunderous steps as Grimrock raced toward Lyrian.

Eila slashed again, capturing Lyrian's attention. This time, she opened his side. Lyrian had twisted aside to avoid a fatal blow, only to find Grimrock careening toward him. Grimrock's mighty fist sent Lyrian soaring out of sight.

Grimrock breathed heavily. "We cannot allow him to escape."

Eila nodded. "I'm not the one who knocked him for six."

Corvus groaned. "Go to him," Eila instructed Grimrock. "I'll find Lyrian."

Grimrock didn't budge.

"Grim!" Eila pressed as the clouds around the storm's eye swirled faster. Something roared. Grimrock reluctantly ran to Corvus and picked him up.

Power thrummed in the clouds, and she felt unsettled as a bright light edged over the distant rocks. She clutched the shield as Lyrian darted into the sky, then conjured a fireball larger than any Eila had never seen. He yelled as he hurled it at her, looking like a comet.

Eila crouched behind the ice shield, but it did not repel the heat. Her clothes singed, and her brow broke out in sweat. She heard Grimrock cry out.

She channeled her augmented power into the shield, and white light swept over it. She thrust the shield forward, and a column of ice battled Lyrian's fire. She rose when the heat receded, and the two energy sources clashed, sparking like fireworks as each fought for dominance.

Eila chanced a glance over her shoulder. Grimrock and Corvus were nowhere to be seen.

While she was distracted, Lyrian pressed the attack. She redoubled the power she sent toward him. He was no longer the faerie she had known. The power had corrupted him, and she couldn't let this world fall into his hands.

"Face it, Eila!" Lyrian called over the crackles and fizzes of the magical battle. "You're done. Your cronies couldn't help you in the end, and this fight will destroy you."

Eila grunted and used her power to jerk Lyrian aside, knocking him off-kilter.

Her mother's words sprang from her mouth. "Sometimes we have to make the greatest sacrifice to save the ones we love."

"It's a shame you'll never see her again. She would be proud of your resolve. You take after her, you know?"

Eila's eyes widened and her knees wobbled as Lyrian gained ground. "You don't know what you're talking about! My mother's dead."

Lyrian laughed. "No, she isn't. I thought you were smarter than that, Eila."

Rage boiled inside Eila. "You're lying!"

"No. Ask your precious queen why your mother never returned."

Eila's anger hit the boiling, and her scream was so loud it hurt her throat. Her power surged at Lyrian, and his eyes widened in alarm when a dark shape appeared behind him. Blazing blue eyes shone from the gloom as a tremendous roar rattled the mountainside.

Eila knew it was over for Lyrian, for her, and maybe for the Faerie realm. Her only regret was that she wouldn't get to see her mother again, since she had just found out she was alive.

Grimrock turned when he saw Lyrian's blast, gathering Corvus to his chest and protecting him. The heat reached levels he had not felt even inside Frostfang's lair. The troll stumbled and fell to one knee.

"Hold tight, Corvus," he warned, but Corvus shrank. In the wavering air, Grimrock could just make out the tiny raven in his hands. He drew the bird closer to him. Corvus was lifeless and light.

And then the next blast of power, so powerful that Grimrock was flung into the air. He tucked into a ball around Corvus and rolled, the relief from the ice and snow brief as he tumbled. Finally, a large rock stopped his advance.

Grimrock lay still for a moment. When he unfurled, he was lying on his back, staring into the power-laced sky. A light show danced above him.

Corvus changed and sat on Grimrock's stomach, hunched. His gaze locked on the red and blue flashes as something monstrous roared in the distance.

"This is it," Corvus managed weakly. "We couldn't stop it. We failed." There was nothing more they could do.

Grimrock mused, "The wheel turns, and the world spins. I have seen it turn for hundreds of years. If my wheel stops turning now, I am glad I have a friend by my side."

Silver tears fell from Corvus' dark eyes. He swallowed dryly, then nodded as his vision came true. Lights sparked and flared as a creature appeared in the sky.

Grimrock gently clasped Corvus' shoulder as the final blast exploded. Another roar deafened them. Eila's shrieks echoed off the mountain as the power threw Grimrock and Corvus in separate directions.

CHAPTER TWENTY-FIVE

The world was now white. The clouds that had been black and gray laced with purple lightning were a bright canvas that hurt the eyes. It was as though all the world's snow was floating above the troll with the sun shining brightly behind it. Was this what the humans meant when they said, "Don't go toward the bright light?" Was he dead?

No, since his body ached for the first time in centuries. It had been almost a thousand years since he'd felt the need to exert himself for so long, and he was paying for it. He grunted, fighting the dazzling light as he sat up, his hands sinking into the snow beneath him.

Where am I?

His back felt strange, but he couldn't reach it or turn his head enough to see it. He was surrounded by rocky spikes, as though he had landed in a meteor crater. Through the only gap, a path led toward a peak. Something white and blue glimmered on its crest.

A handful of snow-white birds flew overhead in a V, their leader crying loudly as they passed.

Grimrock blinked, struggling to focus. Recent events came

back slowly: the storm, the battle, the Summer Fae with dark intentions. He looked around but was unable to see Eila or find Corvus. He was barely able to stand.

This is going to make one hell of a story, he thought as he took cautious steps up the slope, the light still painful. How long had he been out? What had roared after the blast?

Grimrock focused on placing one foot in front of the other. As he walked, he scanned his surroundings, hoping to see Eila or Corvus' feet, wings, or hands sticking out of the snow, but he saw only snow and rock.

Something large loomed ahead of him. It was a dragon.

Frostfang stood at the Crest of the Gods, wings stretched wide. Against the white peak, he was almost invisible. His head swayed as he gazed at someone in front of him, who was also difficult to see, given the white armor the person wore.

Eila.

Grimrock quickened his pace, stumbling as he closed on the peak. Eila turned at the sound of his footsteps, looking considerably the worse for wear. She had dark circles under her eyes, her hair was disheveled, and her clothing was burned and torn.

She was smiling.

"Grim!" Eila called, darting to her friend. She wrapped her arms around his thick neck, grunting when her body met his hard flesh. Grimrock embraced her too tightly, and Eila moaned, then laughed.

"Easy there, big guy. I didn't go through all that to be crushed by a friend."

Grimrock released her. She beamed at him. "You're okay!"

"I am." Grimrock's gaze went to Frostfang, who now studied them both. "Should I be concerned by the presence of a dragon atop the mountain?"

Frostfang chuckled. "Only if you covet the Heart of Frostfire. If you are a friend of the realm, you have nothing to fear."

"He's proven that," Eila returned, admiration and affection in her eyes. Before Grimrock could ask follow-up questions, Eila added, "Grim, have you seen Corvus?"

The troll's heart sank. He looked around as if he might see Corvus waving. "No. He got separated from me in the blast. I…" The memory returned, the light so bright and the magic so powerful that the raven had fallen out of his hands. "I don't know where he is."

Eila frowned. "Frostfang, I know you said that dragons typically don't interfere in mortal affairs, but do you think you could help us now?"

Frostfang shook his head, his body rippling. "You know I cannot. I must return to my cavern and protect the jewel that can change the world. You must bear your burdens alone."

Without another word, Frostfang took to the air, sending up snow and debris. Grimrock, who had seen many things in his long life, marveled as the dragon rose. One minute he was visible, and the next, his white scales blended with the sky and he was gone.

When the Heart was gone, Eila's armor disappeared.

Grimrock looked at her for answers. He couldn't understand why the dragon had come, then left so quickly.

Sensing his questions, Eila replied, "I'll explain later. We have to find Corv."

Grimrock nodded and turned his attention to the mountainside.

Eila wasn't sure how long they searched. Time was a blur, and so was the mountainside, the white and gray of one side blending in with the white and gray of the other as they scoured the landscape for signs of their companion.

Her heart thumped, and she idly touched her chest as though the Heart of Frostfire were still there. She beat her wings, fighting Lyrian's damage to stay upright. After a while, she spotted a body in the snow.

She didn't call Grimrock, just flew over and landed beside the crumpled body. Lyrian.

Eila's anger burned, mixed with a grief she couldn't process. The items Lyrian had stolen were still on his body, and as panic for Corvus set in, she put the Verdant Crystal and the Sunfire Amulet around her neck and the Crown on her head, and clutched the Sceptre in her shaking hands. After she flew away, she didn't look back.

Minutes passed, and life returned to the skies. Eila frightened a flock of birds as they returned to their nests on the mountainside.

Grimrock cried, *"Eila! Here!"*

Eila almost missed the troll among the rocks until something glimmered on his back. The rocks over his spine had become gemstones, the flames so powerful they had changed Grimrock's body. Greens and purples and blues covered his back, sparkling in the sun.

She darted toward him and gasped when she saw Corvus lying face-down, his body looking small in the snow. Eila rolled him over. His face was as white as the snow around him, and he wasn't breathing. Panic overtook her as she unceremoniously slapped his cheeks and called for him to wake up.

Grimrock stepped back, sadness and sympathy in his eyes. If Eila had turned, she would have seen a tear leave the troll's eyes —the first in centuries.

"Corvus!" Eila called, clutching the lifeless ravenkin to her. "Wake up. Wake *up!*"

She kneeled beside him, and her tears flowed. The Harvest Crown's nuts and berries glowed, and the light passed through Eila into Corvus. She leaned back as the magic took effect. His dark veins faded, and the bags under his eyes vanished. His hair changed from black to white, starting at the roots and spreading to the tips.

Eila turned to Grimrock. "What is happening?"

Grimrock mulled that, the tear lost in his craggy face. "The Harvest Crown is a cleanser that breaks curses. Isn't that what Fenris said?"

"That was the duplicate," Eila replied.

"It was based on the relic."

When the transformation was complete, Corvus looked like a different person. His blond hair contrasted with the black clothing he wore.

Eila studied Corvus' face. "He's not breathing. Grim, he's not breathing."

Grimrock placed two fingers to his lips and blew a long, loud whistle that echoed off the surrounding peaks.

Stamping hooves announced Blizzard's presence.

The snowstrider thundered up the slope and halted next to Grimrock. The troll peeled Corvus out of Eila's grasp and placed him over the snowstrider's back.

"We must hurry," Grimrock stated. "Find Fenris at Aria's safe house and summon him to Nemora. There is little time to spare. I do not know if the curse of death can be broken as easily as that of the ravenkin, but we must try. Go. I will meet you there."

A thousand questions flickered through Eila's mind, but her body acted without it. She took to the sky, her flight clumsy and awkward as she raced down the mountain, using gravity to move faster.

Tears froze on her face as she followed Grimrock's instructions, hoping that she made it to Fenris in time, and that Queen Amara and her soldiers wouldn't find and detain her before she could save her friend.

CHAPTER TWENTY-SIX

Waiting was painful. She had found Fenris and brought him to Nemora, but they arrived before Grimrock.

"Patience, Eila," Fenris soothed, the Crystal Pool foaming beside them. "Time might have no effect on what is to come."

Was Fenris saying they could save Corvus, or that it was over, and further effort would be futile?

She bounced on her toes, eyes fixed on the trail as she waited for Grimrock to arrive with the ravenkin. She had raced across the Winter Court after finding Aria in a place she and Eila knew all too well. She had given her friend the Icicle Sceptre, wrapped in a cloth from the village leader's house, and sent her to return the Sceptre to the queen.

On Glisten's back, Eila and Fenris had sped to the Faerie Door Eila had been banished through, half-expecting to find Grimrock and Corvus on the way. They had left Glisten at the top. Eila had instructed him to find his way back to Agnes before emerging into the stink caused by London's waterways.

Along the way, she had told Fenris what had occurred at the Crest of the Gods. He had been silent throughout their journey.

When they reached the Green Dragon, Fenris left Thrumble and the others and took Eila with him to the secret realm.

Eila just wanted to see Corvus' face one more time, dead or alive. "They're not coming. Something happened to Grim."

"He'll come," Fenris sounded confident.

How did he know? Did his third eye see that happening? Eila fidgeted, and her breath caught when someone emerged from the forest. Grimrock walked swiftly, carrying Corvus as he approached the pool.

"Grim, hurry," Eila called, although several hours had passed since they recovered Corvus from the mountainside.

The troll crouched beside the pool, and at Fenris' gesture, lowered Corvus into the water.

"Release him," Fenris instructed, eyes fixed on the ravenkin's body.

Grimrock allowed Corvus to float. Eila's heart ached at how pale her friend's face was.

Corvus sank, and Eila's worry increasing as he drifted deeper into the pool.

She moved to jump in, but Fenris stopped her. "Wait." He stepped to the edge, removed his crown, and placed it on the pool's surface. It floated and bobbed like a paper boat. He turned to Eila and motioned for her to crouch.

"The Crystal," Fenris coached, nodding at the Verdant Crystal around Eila's neck.

Eila removed the Crystal and dipped it in the water. As soon as it touched the pool, the crystal glowed bright green.

"A crown to heal, a Crystal for re-birth," Fenris stated, motioning for Eila to remove her crown.

She did, concern flaring in her eyes as Corvus sank deeper.

The two crowns floated like lazy ducks as the Crystal brightened. Green power floated down toward Corvus in a thick trail and wrapped around his body like a vine. It drew him up to the surface, green light radiating through his body.

Corvus gasped, and his back arched as his eyes snapped open. His chest rose as he looked wildly around, unable to process what was happening.

"What the..." he began. There was a flash, and he had to flail his arms to stay afloat. He spun in the water, looking from the smiling Grimrock to the stoic Fenris to the beaming Eila.

"Eila—" Corvus started.

Eila jumped into the pool, wrapped her arms around his neck, and pressed her lips to his. He was stunned, but he closed his eyes. They kicked in rhythm to stay afloat.

Grimrock eyed Fenris, who smirked. "I've never seen that before."

"The healing, or the kissing?" Grimrock asked.

Fenris laughed and turned around. Gizmo stood in the tunnel, looking curious. Fenris waved a hand. "Don't ask."

Gizmo glanced at Grimrock, then followed Fenris into the workshop.

Eila missed the byplay. She held Corvus, finally beginning to believe things would be okay.

One more stop and we'll return this.

Eila flew through London with the bundle beneath her jacket. The pool had healed her wing, and fresh energy coursed through her body.

The Fenris' Harvest Crown had special abilities. Now, she had the *true* Crown, and as she flew in the golden glow of dawn, she understood the power of the relics. Was the idea that had entered her head after Corvus was healed selfish? She didn't think so.

Corvus silently fluttered beside her, lost in his thoughts. Occasionally, Eila glanced at him, heart stopping as she imagined Lyrian beside her. Although he was still the person she knew and loved, minus the curse, the blond hair took some getting used to.

They had to evade Oathkeepers before they reached Under the Bridge, but they touched down outside the familiar rundown entry building shortly thereafter. As she went down the stairs and into the library, she cupped her hands and called, "Jim? Wake up! I have a present for you."

Ozzie was slithering across the books on Grimrock's tables, leaving damp trails. Jim appeared through a doorway, rubbing his eyes. "What the hell? It's the middle of the night."

"It's morning," Eila corrected, "but forget that. I've got a surprise for you." She held the Harvest Crown in front of her.

Jim glanced between the crown and Eila and Corvus. When his gaze settled on the ravenkin, his brows knitted. "Blond doesn't suit you, dude. Go back to black. You're not Eminem."

Corvus' lips thinned.

"Just hold this." Eila thrust the Harvest Crown into Jim's hands. She wondered whether a naïve human had ever held something so powerful.

Jim examined the crown. "Nice. You woke me up to give me a kindergarten gift. What is it, a bird's nest? There's a hole in the middle."

"Put it on your head," Eila instructed.

Jim obeyed. It looked absurd. "Great. Now what?"

"Shut up for a minute," Eila replied. They all stood with bated breath, Eila watching for a sign that the Crown was activating. When she was about to give up hope, the red berries twinkled.

Jim shuddered. "What *was* that?"

Eila smiled as she removed the crown. "Lie to me."

"Huh?"

"Tell me your name."

"Jim."

Eila shot an exasperated glance at Corvus.

"How many women have you slept with in your lifetime?" Corvus asked. Eila scoffed.

"Like, fifty," Jim shot back. He paused, eyes widening. "Ho-ly shit."

Corvus smirked. "I figured."

"I can lie again?" Jim chortled. *"I can lie again!"*

Eila rolled her eyes. "The curse is gone." She bowed. "You're welcome."

To her surprise, Jim wrapped his arms around Eila and spoke into her collarbone, sobbing. "Thank you so much, Eila. Thank you."

Eila exchanged glances with Corvus.

"Don't go back to your old ways," Eila warned. "Do better, okay? *Be* better. Corvus and I will be watching. Pull your former shit, and I'll curse you again, and next time, I doubt I'll be able to get my hands on this item to fix you."

Jim pulled free, wiping a tear from his eyes. "Thank you, Eila. Thank you so much. I might be able to build a proper life now."

Eila looked at the crown. "We should get this back to Fenris. It's time to restore the faerie kingdoms' balance." Holding hands, she and Corvus returned to the park and flew into the dusk to finish what they'd started.

EPILOGUE

Banished...

Eila remembered standing in the center of the throne room under the withering glares of the Seven. Back then, she had thought she would never return to the Winter Court, set foot in the Winter Palace, or look into Queen Amara's eyes again.

Yet, here she was.

Eila stood on the spot where she had been sentenced for freeing Lyrian. This time, as she stared into Queen Amara's cool, emotionless eyes, she was not alone. Corvus and Grimrock flanked her. Fenris had been invited as well, his reputation preceding him since he had returned the relics to their kingdoms.

A team of outcasts, invited to the palaces from which they were exiled.

Corvus shifted closer to Eila. He shivered, and his breath misted before him. He looked dashing with blond hair, but he still wore black fatigues.

Over the past couple of days, as they restored the kingdoms' equilibrium, she hadn't spent as much time with Corvus as she'd have liked. When the waters of the Crystal Pool had washed away the corruption, it had also removed the curse. Now, instead of a raven's, Corvus sported elegant fae wings. Rather than harnessing the shadows and the darkness and transfiguring into a raven, Corvus had Winter fae powers.

Since that day, the glimmer in his eye had faded. Although he sounded upbeat, Eila knew something was missing.

"My valued friends," Queen Amara began from the throne. Eila had been surprised to find that Silas had been replaced by a familiar face. Her father looked her way without emotion, and her heart fluttered. Aria had confirmed that the charges had been dropped.

"Welcome to the Winter Palace," Queen Amara continued. "On behalf of every faerie in this court, thank you for your recent services and deeds."

The Seven bowed their heads in gratitude.

Eila glanced at Corvus and Grimrock. Her comrades kept their gazes on the queen, but Corvus' hand found hers.

"Mightier deeds have rarely been seen," the queen continued, "and I extend the gratitude of all four Faerie kingdoms. As much as it pains me to say this, without your blatant insubordination," her eyes flashed to Eila, "and complete disregard for your actions, we might be on the brink of calamity. We acknowledge your bravery. Your deeds will be recorded for the generations to come."

Eila stepped forward, drawing the courtiers' attention. "It was not service to this kingdom that propelled us to act," she started, and the temperature dropped a few degrees. Her father shot her a wary look to warn her not to speak so freely.

Queen Amara was silent, but her lips had a bemused twist.

"It was for all the kingdoms," Eila pressed, "and every person with a droplet of good in them. Mostly," she motioned at Fenris and the other two, "it was so my friends could live in a world in which they would not have to fear.

"And if there are repercussions for our rule breaking, I will shoulder the punishment for all. I could not have done what I did without the brave and selfless deeds of these people and more, but I was the instigator, so I will gladly make reparations."

"Eila, no," Corvus whispered.

The queen raised her hand to quiet Corvus as her Seven shifted uncomfortably. For a moment, the room was silent. Finally, Amara stood and slowly walked forward. She was shorter than Eila, but her aura of command and authority befit her royal status. Her elegant gown trailed in her wake, rippling like water.

When she stopped, Corvus squeezed Eila's fingers.

"You are a fighter, I see," the queen told Eila admiringly. "A warrior. Although many speak of bravery, few follow through. Without faeries like you, the kingdom would be overrun with enemies." Her next words were so quiet that the Seven had to strain to hear her. "There will be no punishment, Eila Snowshadow. I won't punish anyone who put their lives on the line for their kingdom."

She gazed at Eila's companions. "You four heroes will each be granted a boon, although I cannot not do miracles. Please, take a moment to decide what you want."

Queen Amara glided back to the throne. When she sat, the courtiers started chattering.

Eila turned to the others. "I know what I will ask for. How about you?"

They glanced at each other, none saying what they wanted. Sensing their discomfort, Eila asked, "Your Highness, could we ask for our gifts in private? I believe they are of a sensitive nature."

"Not mine," Corvus stated, eagerly stepping forward.

The queen turned her gaze upon him. "Very well. State your wish."

Corvus stood straight, steeling himself. Eila would never have predicted his wish. "I wish to be cursed again." Corvus laced his fingers behind his back.

"You wish to be cursed?" The queen shifted in her seat. "I do not know what you are requesting."

"Restore the ravenkin curse. That will make me feel complete again."

The Seven bristled.

Corvus continued. "After the battle, my curse was removed by the Harvest Crown and the Crystal Pool. For a short while, I thought that was a good thing. But this?" He twisted to display his faerie wings. "This is not who I was born to be or am, and despite the curse and the shame on my family's legacy, I proudly wear the badge of the raven upon my skin." He looked at the queen earnestly. "That is my request. Please, your Majesty."

The queen considered. Eila thought she would dismiss Corvus' request, but Amara stood, raised a hand, and closed her eyes. Gleaming white power from her palm flew toward Corvus in a rippling ribbon.

He gasped when it touched him. His faerie wings dissolved, and his hair turned black again. Corvus inspected himself.

Eila beamed. This was the Corvus she knew and loved. "You look dashing," she whispered, and he smiled.

Corvus closed his eyes and changed to raven form, then flew around the throne room. The Seven tensed, prepared to defend the queen, but he landed beside Eila again.

Eila and her father exchanged delighted glances.

The queen stated, "Please decide who will be the next to receive a boon, and be quick about it. I have a kingdom to run."

The queen dismissed the Seven, and the party decided Eila would make the next request. Corvus, Grimrock, and Fenris followed the Seven into the hall.

Eila waited for the door to close. In the now-quiet throne room, she could hear her heart beating.

"Approach," the queen ordered.

Eila stepped toward Amara, stopping just short of the throne.

"My, what a journey you embarked on," the queen began. "My people are forever in your debt, Eila Snowshadow."

"Your people are my people, too," Eila returned.

The queen looked thoughtful. "They were, but I cannot repeal your banishment. Although you showed great heroism, that would send the wrong message to my court."

Eila's brow furrowed. "That was not what I was going to ask, but thanks for making that clear."

The queen's gaze bored into Eila's. "What do you wish, then?"

Eila looked at the floor, then at the doorway through which her father had exited. For a moment, images of her mother in the frozen woods and at the hearth came to her. She thought about Silas' contempt for her family and the suggestions he had delivered regarding her mother in his final moments.

Lyrian's final words rang in her mind: *Ask your precious queen what happened to her. Ask her why your mother never returned.*

Eila did.

D.S. BAILEY'S NOTES

FEBRUARY 7, 2025

Oh my, oh my.

We're back, and this time we've gone on a little trip to Faerie.

I had a lot of fun with this one. Don't get me wrong, it's great holding up a mirror to the human world and thinking, "Hmm... how can we twist and bend the familiar to squeeze in a little magic?"

But it's rare I get the chance to dive into the completely fantastical.

Fans of fantasy may already have had their preconceptions about Faerie. I know there's *some* literature out there that has coloured in some of the pages and shown what Faerie *could* be.

But this is *our* Faerie. By taking some of the common tropes and details, I drew in the edges of the picture, then allowed myself to have a little fun.

Snowstriders, glowberries, mooncalves...it all sounds so magical, doesn't it? It was a blast traipsing the gang out into the wilds on their quest, and when the stakes are this high, what better setting than to throw Eila back into the cold with the law on her heels?

These last three books have been an honour to write, and

would *not* have been written without the incredible guidance and help of the LMBPN team: Kelly, Lynne, Tracey, Grace, David and, of course, Michael.

What Michael has created at LMBPN is nothing short of a miracle. The fact that I've had the chance to read so many books from my favourite writers—and write among them—is insanity to me. This year (2025) will be my tenth year as a published author, and part of that for me has been reflection on the last decade and my journey. I still have a memory, clear as day, of asking if Michael needed any more collaborators, and the nervousness that sprang when he asked to jump on a call one evening.

I was living with my ex-partner at the time, a four-year-old running around my legs. I stepped into the conservatory (my office at the time), and jumped on a call with Michael, LE Barbant, and CM Raymond, with discussions about contributing some zombies to the Kurtherian's "Age of Madness."

I jumped at the chance. There are five books in The Caitlin Chronicles (in case you haven't read them yet). I've had the chance to work on a number of projects with Michael through the years and I'm always bowled over by his generosity, ideas, and the efforts of the whole team.

So, all of that to say, thank you everyone at LMBPN for all you've done over the last few years of my writing, and for entertaining so many readers.

I think we can all say we're lucky to live in such times.

Except for, maybe, Eila. Because somewhere out there, I'm afraid I feel the darkness growing.

Daniel Willcocks (D.S. Bailey)

MICHAEL'S NOTES

JANUARY 31, 2025

First, thank you for not only reading this story but also venturing into these author notes tucked away at the end.

Second, thank you to my collaborator and the editor for making this story happen!

Salisbury Steak Kicked My Ass

I appreciate you hanging out to hear my latest confession: *I, Michael Anderle, do hereby proclaim defeat in my quest to cook homemade Salisbury steak in a slow cooker.*

I've tried—oh, I've tried. I bought this slow cooker a while back, convinced that if I can craft epic battles in my stories, *I can certainly conquer a simple meal.* How hard could it be, right? It turns out, very.

I mean, I can't even match the taste of the budget-friendly, store-bought frozen versions that turn out pretty damn tasty (looking at you, Stouffer's).

Not only is this fiasco hitting my pride, it's also hitting my wallet. The money I've thrown at three separate attempts could've fed me for two weeks (incl. drinks) with the microwavable variety. The worst part? Even with all the time, groceries, and vivid imagination, I still can't replicate that cheap-but-delicious gravy-laden Salisbury steak flavor I secretly crave. (Don't judge!)

In the spirit of full disclosure and because apparently, I like sharing my repeated kitchen failures, I've also bombed cubed steak and gravy. Go figure. Those convenient $9.99 ready-made packages at the store are starting to look more like five-star dining compared to my lumps of tough meat and questionable sauces.

I'm only slightly afraid to check the ingredients list (and by "slightly," I mean I'd rather remain blissfully ignorant.) Maybe those preservatives will keep me looking brand-new in my coffin someday.

Silver linings, right?

It's embarrassing, but hey, I'm barreling ahead, determined to make at least a few slow cooker triumphs before I throw the crockpot out the window. (Then again, that vacuum sealer I bought might make me feel better about my leftover shame. Might as well store my failures for another day, am I right?)

Anyway, thank you for humoring my rant on my not-so-epic Salisbury steak saga. Next time you see me, hopefully I'll be crowing about a new recipe I didn't ruin—or maybe I'll just have a suspiciously large stock of prepackaged meals. Whichever way the spatula flips, I'm glad you're here, traveling this wacky culinary road with me.

Until we meet again in the back of another book, keep reading, keep cooking (way better than me, I hope), and let's look forward to more story worlds where maybe the characters can cook better than their creator.

Ad Aeternitatem,
    Michael Anderle

P.S. If you've managed to create a half-decent slow cooker Salisbury steak (or if you just want to share your favorite prepackaged meal hacks), I'm all ears. And if you enjoy the occasional random rant, don't forget to join the MORE STORIES with Michael newsletter: https://michael.beehiiv.com/

P.S.S. Stay tuned for our next adventure—whether it's in the kitchen, among the stars, or somewhere in between. I promise at least one of those worlds will have better food than mine!

BOOKS FROM D.S. BAILEY

Eila's Exile
Banished (Book One)
Blacking (Book Two)
Frostfire (Book Three)

The Caitlin Chronicles
(written as Daniel Willcocks)
Dawn of Chaos (Caitlin Chronicles Book 1)
Into the Fire (Caitlin Chronicles Book 2)
Hunting the Broken (Caitlin Chronicles Book 3)
The City Revolts (Caitlin Chronicles Book 4)
Chasing the Cure (Caitlin Chronicles Book 5)

CONNECT WITH THE AUTHORS

Connect with D.S. Bailey (Dan Willcocks)

Website: www.danielwillcocks.com/eila

Instagram: https://www.instagram.com/willcocksauthor

Connect with Michael Anderle

Website: http://lmbpn.com

Email List: https://michael.beehiiv.com/

https://www.facebook.com/LMBPNPublishing

https://twitter.com/MichaelAnderle

https://www.instagram.com/lmbpn_publishing/

https://www.bookbub.com/authors/michael-anderle

OTHER LMBPN PUBLISHING BOOKS

To be notified of new releases and special promotions from LMBPN publishing, please join our email list:

http://lmbpn.com/email/

For a complete list of books published by LMBPN please visit the following pages:

https://lmbpn.com/books-by-lmbpn-publishing/

BOOKS BY MICHAEL ANDERLE

Sign up for the LMBPN email list to be notified of new releases and special deals!

https://lmbpn.com/email/

For a complete list of books by Michael Anderle, please visit:

www.lmbpn.com/ma-books/

www.ingramcontent.com/pod-product-compliance
Lightning Source LLC
LaVergne TN
LVHW041936070526
838199LV00051BA/2814